THE GUARDIAN DOLPHIN

K. R. WATTS

STUART TARTLY PRESS

Stuart Tartly Press
17216 Saticoy Street, #226
Lake Balboa, CA 91406-2103

ISBN: 978-1-7337402-0-3

FREE BOOK

If you enjoy this book, go to krwatts.com/TGD-P to get your free copy of another book by K. R. Watts

To Virginia

But I am not to say it is a sea, for it is now the sky:
between the firmament and it you cannot thrust a
bodkin's point.

— WILLIAM SHAKESPEARE

F orty, fifty years, and I still remember the sunset, the color of the sea.

Picture this:

Sea and sky, as far as the eye can see. Clouds tinged with sunset, salt in the air, the lap of a wave, the cry of a gull.

Silence.

A young dolphin, smooth skin gleaming, comes out of the water—quick, clean, alive—hangs for a moment against the sunset, then plunges back into the waves.

Into the thick green reaches of the deep, a liquid space where you hear the rocks, the seaweed, the fish—hear them more clearly than you can see.

You push downward, your tail driving you into darkness, into pressure, right through a school of bass. Nothing else matters, nothing. You push as far as you dare, past coral, past rocks, and when you've reached your absolute limit, you turn in a nice broad circle to maintain your speed and drive upward again.

This time the pressure of the sea is behind you, the urgency in your lungs drives you, every muscle, every sinew, strains for the surface and beyond. You fasten on the light with your mind, reel it in, drive yourself upward with tail, with torso. It rushes closer, closer, and still you push until you think you will burst, and then...

You break through, into the light, into the sky. You soar higher, cleaner, freer than ever, and you know.

It is going to happen.

It runs through your body like like magic, like time. It turns you inside out, fills you with hope and pain. The sounds turn to light and you are transformed.

My lower body split in half. My fins became long and spindly—the ends branching into fingers. One moment I was a sleek, muscular dolphin. The next I was elbows and knees and fear. I hung ten feet above the waves, a nine-year-old human, a boy. And then I began to fall.

I hit belly first. My fins didn't work. My breathing hole had moved. I couldn't find the surface.

The water had never been my enemy before.

I finally got my head—I had a separate head now—into the air. I managed something like a dog-paddle.

Then something lifted me. I looked over my shoulder. An enormous wall of water towered over me. It hurled me toward shore with sand in my mouth and foam in my eyes, slamming me against the bottom, spinning me, roaring in my ears, stinging my throat, until, finally, it flung me onto the beach.

The water drained away from the wet sand before my eyes. I lay naked, shivering. I didn't know how to control this strange new body. After a time I managed to turn my head to the side. The beach stretched out forever, and there—so far that I could barely make him out—came Charlie.

I lay terrified as he limped toward me, step by painful step. Finally he was closer than I'd seen a human before.

He was a wiry old man in faded army fatigues, his remaining hair in a crewcut. He had limped without a sign of hurry, and didn't slow as he came close. I was afraid he would step on me, and winced as he stopped, towering over me.

He pushed his lips out, like a puckerfish, and whistled.

Then he spoke.

"It's been so long. I thought there wouldn't be any more."

Good old Charlie.

THE TRAVELING ANGEL

1

THE HOGAN CASE

I want to tell you a story.

Part of it is mine; part is only mine to tell.

Don't ask why it happened this way.

Don't ask how I know.

You might as well ask why a baby smiles—how the right woman brings meaning with her, like a shawl.

It's magic, that's all.

Like yesterday.

Like everything.

Like the color of the sea.

I sat in my usual spot, at the Seaside Bar and Grill, staring out the window at the surfers below.

It was early afternoon. The place was empty except for me and Kels, all three hundred pounds of him, behind the bar.

The sunlight and salt air tumbled through the open window, carrying the sound of gulls.

Half of me was thinking that some days California really was paradise, and the other half was remembering that evening I first met Charlie.

A dolphin surfaced just beyond the breakers and called toward shore.

It's funny how these things happen.

The call didn't cause me any physical pain, but I still couldn't bear it. I shrank away from the window, then grabbed the sill and slammed it down, sealing myself in the bar.

I'd never felt that way before, but I knew exactly what it meant. The heat drained from my blood, and I gave a single, violent shiver.

Kels glanced my way at the sound, rolled his eyes, and went back to his inventory.

The dolphin was still calling to me, silently, from the other side of the glass.

I leaned forward.

The sun played across my face, and the reflection of an old man stared back at me from the window.

An impressive old man, to be sure: I still had a full head of hair, gray but curly. I sported a distinguished goatee with a few flecks of black offsetting the silver. I only wore the glasses for style—I didn't need a prescription. I had a sparkle in my eye and a bounce in my step, but I was, undeniably, old.

Old enough to have made my mark on the world. Old enough to know who I was. Old enough to have nothing more to prove.

How long had it been?

I couldn't remember.

I thought of opening the window again, just a crack—but I didn't.

Instead, I pushed my chair back and looked at Kels. He was messing with the remote control for the television over the bar.

"I'm going back, Kels."

He looked up. "Back?"

"Before it's too late."

He raised those black eyebrows of his, thought about it, then nodded.

"Good for you."

I had no idea whether Kels believed I was a dolphin. I'd told him the story a hundred times—all about the first time I changed into a human, all about Charlie finding me on the beach. I'd told Kels my whole life story, for that matter. He always listened patiently, raised his eyebrows, stared at the bar top—or the glass he was polishing with his stubby fingers—and made interested noises.

He probably thought I was nuts.

"This going to be a formal swim?" He was looking my way again.

"What?"

He nodded at my garment bag, hanging over the back of a chair.

"Because you have a tab, you know."

"I'm just going to change here, later."

"I see."

"I've got some things to do before I go," I said. "I can't just run off and leave a bunch of loose ends, can I?"

He shook his head and aimed the remote control at the TV.

I stood up.

"Wait!" I said. "I want to see this."

It was *The Bishop's Wife*, old Charlie's favorite movie.

The first scene is great.

It's Christmas time, the shop windows are crammed with toys, and a group of carolers sing on the street. Sidewalk Santas ring their bells, snow is falling, and Cary Grant strolls, smiling, through it all. He's an angel, named Dudley, sent to help people in distress.

He takes the arm of a blind man trying to cross an intersection. The blind man smiles.

"Oh, this is very kind of you," the blind man says.

"It's a privilege," says Dudley.

They cross the street, and this beautiful heavenly music swells the air as the cars miraculously stop on either side.

God, I loved that movie.

If I had only known.

I grabbed a handful of peanuts at the bar, and filled Kels in on the plot.

"Cary Grant is an angel," I explained. "He just travels around helping people out."

"I've seen the movie. You ever consider buying anything?"

"So many people need help, you know? Need a Traveling Angel."

Kels moved the peanuts out of reach. He's a bit anal.

The next scene was just as good. This little boy asks his mother to lift him up, so he can see the toys. She lifts him, and her baby carriage—with the baby in it—rolls down the sidewalk behind her, right in front of a truck.

Old Charlie had no psychic distance. This scene used to make him jump, even after he'd seen it five times.

But that beautiful music plays again, the truck screeches to a halt, and—you guessed it—Dudley appears, just in time to grab the baby carriage. The woman rushes up to thank him, but Dudley simply smiles.

"Just don't let it happen again. Now on your way."

"Dressing up?"

Kels was looking at my garment bag again. I glanced around to make sure no one was listening, then I leaned forward and whispered.

"I'm wrapping up the Hogan case tonight."

"Hogan case." He squinted at me. "You got *cases* now?"

I ignored his sarcasm, pulled the newspaper out of my coat pocket, and showed him the picture on the front page. It was a group of people standing in front of a framed circus poster. Kels frowned and read the headline.

"Local Developers Got Their Start with Circus—So?"

"Not so loud." I said.

He glanced one way and then the other, bobbing his head a little the whole time, then turned his weary eyes back on me.

"There's only the two of us in the room."

I lowered my voice anyway, and pointed at the man to the left of the poster.

"That's William Hogan. He wants to run an oil pipeline through the bay. The others are his investors."

"I know who William Hogan is. What do you have to do with this?"

TELL ME ABOUT WILLIAM AND YOU

"That pipeline's a bad idea, Kels. Bad for the bay, bad for the town, bad for the beaches."

Kels nodded at me, pursing his lips.

"What you gonna do this time?"

"There's a big party tonight at Hogan's. He plans to have them all sign the papers. He doesn't know there's a Traveling Angel on the job."

"A traveling angel."

It was a comment, not a question. Kels talks like that. I just kept going.

"I've already convinced his sister Betty to pull her money out—that's her, the good-looking woman beside William. And Larry—the guy with the mustache—he's wavering, too. Afraid of bad publicity."

"How is Mr. Hogan going to feel about all this?"

"Oh, he'll thank me."

"Like Mrs. Johnson?"

"That wasn't my fault."

"Or that salesman last year?"

"A fluke. I've got the touch. Believe me, Kels, he's going to thank me."

"Hi."

It was Betty, William's sister, standing right behind me. I grabbed the paper back from Kels, stuffed it in my pocket, and smiled, trying to figure out how much she could have heard.

"Betty! What a surprise! Is something wrong?"

She shrugged as though it was nothing.

"I've been thinking about William's project—pulling my money out, like you said. I'm not sure I can do this to him."

It was time for the Traveling Angel to move into action. I put on my most reassuring face.

"Kelsey, this is Betty, William Hogan's sister. Pour her a scotch."

"No, thanks." Betty shook her head.

I nodded for Kels to go ahead and pour anyway. He raised his eyebrows at me, but he did it.

I moved Betty to the sofa Kels kept by the front door.

I smiled.

"Come," I said. "Let's sit down."

I sat beside her.

"Now tell me about William and you. Tell me."

"William and me? I don't know what you mean. He's my brother..."

"About William, then. What worries you about him?"

"Look, I know how important this is to you. I admit the pipeline's wrong—"

"You think that's what this is about? The pipeline? That's not what this is about."

"It isn't?"

"What William's trying to do, Betty, is prove himself. He's trying to be this tycoon—this person he isn't—in order to earn his right to be here."

"You think so?"

"He's lost touch with himself. He needs—he desperately needs—to get away, to—"

And right at that moment, in the middle of a sentence, when I needed every bit of concentration to reel her in, Kels opened the window.

That damn dolphin was still calling to me.

I tried to ignore it, to focus on Betty. I pulled my thoughts together. What was I saying?

"...he needs... William needs..."

I couldn't think what William needed. All I could think about was that grinding dolphin call, the endless "*chirp, chirp, chirp.*"

"...William needs to take a break," I said. "...to find himself again," I said. "to... to..."

To what?

"*Chirp, chirp...*"

"...to get back in touch..." I said, "to..."

The chirping stopped. I breathed a sigh of relief.

Betty looked worried.

"Are you all right?"

"What was I saying?"

"About William," she prompted. "Needing to take a break."

"To get back in touch." I found the thread. "Yes. Exactly. And we're going to give him that chance. Tonight."

She wasn't convinced.

"Come on, Betty. You know how he's been lately. He thinks he knows what's best for everyone."

I dropped my voice to a whisper.

"He plots behind people's backs, has secret conversations..."

I glanced around the room, then leaned closer.

"Don't mention this conversation to him. It's for his own good. A few more hours, it'll be over. He'll thank us."

Betty sighed. "I just can't do it. I'm sorry, but I promised him."

She stood up, flashed a smile at Kels, and left.

Behind the bar, Kels grinned at me like he'd had a thousand-dollar hour.

"What?" I demanded.

He pointed to the television.

"I'd forgotten about this part," he said. "You're just in time."

It was still *The Bishop's Wife.*

Dudley moved a woman toward a sofa.

He smiled.

"Come," he said. "Let us sit down."

He sat beside her.

"Now tell me about Adam and you, tell me."

Kels raised his eyebrows, but I just shrugged.

I didn't know what the hell he was grinning about.

YELLOW WOULD BE GOOD

I remember the way the sun beat down, mornings, on Charlie's porch. I remember the way old tennis shoes felt, pulled onto bare feet. I remember the sea breeze on my young arms, bare and muscled. They were muscled once, and tanned.

I was sixteen, maybe seventeen, on my way down to the water during summer vacation.

Charlie called after me from the house.

"Hey, Pup!"

I turned and grinned at the old man standing in the open door. He wore a flowered apron over his army surplus shirt and pants, and had a dishrag in one hand. It dripped onto the carpet as he grinned back.

"Yeah, Charlie?"

"Bring a fish home for lunch!"

He winked at our little secret, and I would have laughed out loud if my adolescent pride had let me.

"Sure, Charlie."

"A big one!"

"You got it."

Summers were my favorite time, growing up. I never really

enjoyed school because I never felt at ease with the other kids. I put on a good enough show, I guess, and I wasn't what you'd call unpopular, but I never really knew what to say or how to act, and so I felt different, not really part of the group.

They probably thought it was me who rejected them, but I wouldn't have guessed that at the time.

Summers were different.

I didn't have to hang around the others if I didn't want to, and best of all, I could go down to the beach. I loved the water, the scent of the sea, the crashing waves, the wet sand on bare feet. I loved lying in the sun, swimming in the surf, and, when no one was watching, slipping under a wave and going deep, along the bottom, out to sea.

I almost never bothered to change back to a dolphin for those swims. I could go far enough out without changing, and the change itself took an awful lot of energy. Besides, Charlie had warned me not to do it unless I really needed to. He was always afraid someone would see me.

That morning I hiked to a secluded beach I knew, where I would be alone. I wasn't going to change, but Charlie had asked for a fish, and it's hard to explain walking out of the surf with a catch in your hand.

I swam out beyond the breakers, and dived into the cool green depths. For a while I just enjoyed myself, drifting along the bottom. I heard a whale call—miles away—and watched an octopus stalk a crab. It pounced suddenly, and drove its beak through the poor crab's shell, killing it with poison.

I looked up toward the surface light. Above me I saw what I had come for: a school of sea bass, waving like a silver banner in the current.

I kicked toward them, and, just as they started to shy away, I opened my mouth to let out a blast. A blast—that was what

Charlie and I called it. It's a dolphin sound, so loud and focused it can stun a fish.

I was young then, and could still do that.

The fish closest to me drifted, stunned, in the current. I moved in, picked the best one of the lot, and left the others to recover.

Then I kicked off toward shore.

I cooked the fish myself, in Charlie's old iron skillet. I used bacon fat; I liked it better than Oleo-especially the way it smelled in the pan. The radio played "Ghost Riders", and Charlie limped around the table, setting out jelly glasses and pouring milk.

He didn't seem healthy to me lately.

"That sure smells good, pup. How far out did you have to go?"

"Further than last time. You should have come along."

"Sometime, maybe."

"You never go out anymore, Charlie."

"I know."

"You feeling all right?"

"Sure."

"Your limp is worse."

Charlie hobbled to the window, and stared across the beach.

I waited.

Finally he turned and looked at me.

"It's the virus, Pup. There's nothing I can do about it."

"Don't talk like that, Charlie."

"Got to face facts."

"You should see a doctor."

"A doctor wouldn't have a clue, you know that. Even if there was a cure, it's too late for me."

I decided to change the subject.

"You know, Charlie, we should paint this place."

"Maybe when I first stopped listening to the waves, or to our friends calling from the sea..." He was droning on now, talking more to himself than to me.

"Yellow would be good, to match the linoleum."

"...maybe even the first time I tried to change back and couldn't..."

"We could do it next Saturday..."

"It all happened so fast, one day I was a dolphin, the next..."

"Let's talk about something else, Charlie."

"At first I was desperate. I didn't even notice it happening."

"Please."

"You know what I always thought. I always thought if I really helped one of them it would cure me."

I gnawed on my lower lip and concentrated on frying the fish.

"But I never really did, did I? I was always too selfish, Pup. Too concerned about *me*."

I came out of the restroom at the Seaside Bar and Grill dressed in a dinner jacket, my hair combed, my goatee trimmed, and my fake glasses polished.

The after work crowd had arrived. The place was full of loud voices, laughter—the indefinable sense of relief and celebration people emit when they are finally on their own time.

Things hadn't gone so well with William's sister. It was time to start thinking about plan B.

I crossed to the bar and caught Kels' eye.

"So what do you think?"

He looked me up and down with his mouth pulled to one side.

"Spiffy."

"Thanks."

"You're still sure this is a wonderful idea?"

"You'll see."

"You don't think maybe you should take that little vacation you were talking about first? Rest up a little. Get back in touch?"

"After I take care of this pipeline."

Kels snorted.

"They should be very grateful to you."

He didn't mean it.

I'VE GOT THIS BALANCE GOING

While I was getting ready for his party, William Hogan was in his study—tall, thin, balding, and serious—preparing for the business meeting that night.

He wasn't the kind of man to leave anything to chance.

He had made sure of a thousand details already. The dark wood bookcases had been thoroughly polished. The enormous picture windows that looked out to sea had been washed inside and out. The carpet had been cleaned—not just vacuumed, but cleaned—and there were fresh flowers in the vases.

Now he turned his attention to the meeting itself.

He set up an easel on the large oak study table he normally used for a desk, and placed an artist's sketch of the proposed pipeline—running past a broken down seaside restaurant, across the beach, and into the sea.

William was not happy about the restaurant. That's the way he was. He didn't like anything shabby associated with one of his projects, not even in the background.

The artist had not just included the restaurant in the picture, she had made it look just as bad as it actually was. William would have had her do the sketch over, without the restaurant, but there wasn't time.

He had no choice. That irritated him even more.

He sighed and picked up the contract. It was all there, in order, ready to be duplicated. He had gone over every line, of course, word by word, days ago.

Now he just checked to make sure the pages were all there, and went looking for his housekeeper, to have him make copies for all the principals.

He was halfway to the door when the posters caught his eye.

There were two of them, circus posters, hanging on the wall, side by side in identical frames.

One was an actual printed poster from the "Hogan and Ross Circus", covered with pictures of clowns, acrobats, horses, elephants, tigers and trapeze artists—all in bright colors, leaping, falling, roaring, twisting in mid-air.

The other was just as elaborate, and even more full of promise, but it was handmade. It was the painstaking work of a child, lovingly drawn and lettered and colored, and was now more than a little the worse for wear.

The edges were tattered, the colors faded, the paper yellowed.

It proudly declared that "William and Sam's Circus" would be open "Saturday" in the "field behind William's house, by the old tree."

It was the second poster, the tattered one, which stopped my friend in his tracks that day, even though he had seen it practically every day in the three years since he had hung it there.

Looking at that poster, William remembered a hand-lettered sign announcing "The Great Willini", sitting on a makeshift stage. He remembered the smell of the grass in the field, and the cool morning breeze.

They had made a fortune teller's booth out of sheets and poles. And the ride—they had tied ropes to a wooden crate, and fastened pulleys in the old tree. They had a lemonade stand and a ticket booth.

William had been ten years old.

He had one foot on the tightrope they had stretched between a discarded clothesline pole and a branch of the old tree. His other foot was still planted safely on the thick branch the rope was tied to, and he held a broken broomstick in his hands for balance.

A little blood oozed from the scab on his knee.

He held his breath, and transferred his weight to the rope. His friend Sam watched from the ground.

Then he saw something at the edge of the field.

"Wait, Sam, I'm coming down."

Sam laughed.

"I knew you wouldn't do it."

"In a minute. I will. My dad's over there. Catch."

He tossed the broomstick down to Sam, then dropped to a lower limb. He hung upside-down by his knees for a moment, grabbed the limb with both hands, swung his legs free, and dropped.

"Race you!"

The two sprinted to the driveway, where William's father was just getting out of his car.

William arrived first, panting, to lean nonchalantly against a pine at the edge of the driveway. The poster for "William and Sam's Circus" was tacked to it.

"Well Dad," he said with as much cool as he could muster, "how do you like my circus?"

~

Standing in his study, William glanced down at the contract in his hand. He shook his head, to clear the memories. Then he called for his housekeeper.

"Nick!"

Nick, who was everything William wasn't—short, thickset, amply supplied with hair, and constantly amused—appeared instantaneously.

"Yes?"

"Make sure there are five complete sets here. Tonight is the night. Everything will be signed, sealed, and delivered."

"You got it."

"Signed! Nick! Did my pen come back?"

Nick held up a small box.

"Right here. Good as new."

William pulled the pen from the box and examined it.

It was a fountain pen, the kind with a little lever on the side, so you can fill it from an inkwell. It was not a particularly expensive pen, but it was the one he had signed the first circus contract with, and, after that, almost every contract of importance.

"Excellent. I particularly want my lucky pen tonight: we're signing the deal tonight, and I don't want to take any chances."

One of William's fondest memories was of a top he had as a kid. One of those red wooden things that you wind a string around, all nice and even. Then you throw it, just so, on the summer sidewalk, and pull the string back to make it spin, and it balances on that metal tip, perfectly, like it could go on forever.

Staring at his lucky pen and talking to Nick about the meeting that night, William found himself thinking about that top.

He looked up.

"I've got this balance going, Nick, and I don't want anything —anything—to upset it."

I left the seaside bar and grill—all spruced up for the party and the delicate operation I had to pull off—and walked through the village.

I felt good.

It was Christmas time in a beach town. Shop windows were crammed with toys, and a group of carolers was singing on the street. Sidewalk Santas rang their bells, and I strolled, smiling, through it all.

I came to an old lady who was trying to cross an intersection. She wore a large purple straw hat, and was a little unsteady on her feet. She kept putting one foot off the curb, then pulling it back.

Her daughter, dressed to kill and clearly irritated, stood beside her, kibitzing.

"Mother, the signal is going to change again. If you would just let me help…"

She reached out a hand, but the old lady jerked away.

"I'm not an invalid!" she snapped.

I walked up beside the mother, and spoke without even looking at them.

"You slow down a bit, and everyone starts treating you like a child."

The daughter rolled her eyes, but the old woman understood.

"Exactly," she said, more to the daughter than to me.

I offered an arm.

"Might I have the privilege, ma'am?"

"You certainly may."

"Wonderful!" the daughter said.

It didn't bother me; Kels had made me immune to sarcasm.

The old lady took my arm.

We crossed the street as the cars stopped for the light on either side.

I could have sworn I heard heavenly music.

"Some people know how to listen to a person." The old lady said it to the air.

But the daughter, tagging along behind us, heard her.

"I'll be listening to this for weeks," she said.

While I was playing the Boy Scout in town, William was giving last minute instructions to Nick.

The two of them stood in his study, between the circus posters and the sketch of the pipeline.

"...and tell my nephew to keep his girlfriend away from the study." William said.

He waved a nervous hand in the general direction of the sketch.

"Her mother doesn't want her to know about that pipeline going across their beach."

Nick made a note on his pad and looked up for the next instruction, his face a little too bland. "Anything else?"

William paused, suddenly suspicious.

"Tim's here, isn't he?"

Nick swallowed before answering.

"No."

"No? What do you mean, 'No'?"

"He isn't here yet."

William's hand wandered toward his breast pocket, and the reassuring feel of his lucky pen.

"There, you see? That's what I mean. Little things like that begin to happen, and... and..."

Images of his red top wandered furtively through the recesses of his brain.

"...the equilibrium begins, begins to wobble, and the first thing you know..."

"He'll be here," Nick said. "He's a good kid. He's just a little late, that's all."

William teetered on the edge of panic for a moment, then pulled himself upright. He hated surprises.

"Yeah, well, he'd better have a good excuse, or he won't be spending any more vacations at the beach with me."

The reason William's nephew was late for his duties at the party had dark brown eyes and light brown hair.

Julie was eighteen, slim in a way that made her seem fragile, and would have been quite beautiful if she hadn't always looked so worried.

So I can't blame young Tim for being late.

But at the moment, I was still making my way through town, William was still blaming Tim for being late, and Julie was struggling along a rocky beach in her party dress.

She came to a stop in front of a good-sized boulder—which Tim had clambered over without even slowing down—and wondered exactly how she managed to get into these situations.

If she only knew where they were going, or why. It was her own fault. She should have asked him before they got out of the car.

She contemplated her immediate problem, the boulder directly in front of her. Did she risk her shoes, or take them off and almost certainly get a run in her stockings? Talk about a no-win scenario. Maybe Tim could give her a hand. She called after him.

"Tim! Wait! Come back a minute!"

He turned, already a hundred yards down the beach.

"Come on, we're late already—Uncle William's going to kill me."

No, she hadn't really thought so.

5

I TOSSED MY GIFT

Julie sighed, and yelled after Tim.

"I didn't know we were coming to the beach. I'm not really dressed for this. I'm sorry."

Tim had disappeared around a boulder. His voice drifted back to her.

"Just hurry, okay?"

She decided she'd have to risk her shoes.

When she caught up with him, Tim was leaning on a wall of rock. At about shoulder height there was a short ledge just wide enough to sit or stand on. He grinned. "Here we are!"

Julie didn't have a clue what was expected of her. She looked at the rock, then around the beach below, then out to sea. She nodded, then thinking some response was required, smiled.

"It's very nice," she said.

She knew it was wrong the second it was out of her mouth, but, miraculously, Tim didn't seem to notice. Instead, he put his hands on her hips and turned her so her back was to the rock.

"Jump."

She jumped and he lifted her onto the little ledge.

"Okay, now, sit right there—no, move over just a little—that's right. And lean against this rock."

He stood back and gauged her position, like a photographer setting up a shot.

"Perfect."

"What?"

"Perfect."

He stepped forward and took her hand.

"Now. Julie, will you marry me?"

She laughed. "And live happily ever after?"

"I'm not joking. Will you?"

"You're serious? But, but we only just—you mean it?"

"You can come to LA, and live with me while I finish school. We'll get an apartment."

She ordered her brain to come up with a response, but it wasn't paying attention.

"I'll buy you an engagement ring."

She stifled a giggle.

He was so sincere.

I was still making my way through town.

It was sunset, just dark enough to make the Christmas lights and the shop windows come alive in the orange half-light. The street took on a magic glow.

Exotic scents wafted from the open door of a candle shop.

A few steps ahead of me, a little boy struggled to keep up with his preoccupied mother. She stopped suddenly, to look at some toys in a shop window, and he took the opportunity to drop to the sidewalk and rest his legs.

It reminded me of the scene with Dudley and the baby carriage.

The steady drumming of the evening traffic mingled with the voices of the carolers a block behind me.

I passed the mother and boy and made a sharp turn into the toy shop.

There is absolutely nothing in the world like a really good toy shop—the old-fashioned kind—full of puppets and puzzles and chemistry sets and model trains, and all those wooden and rubber gadgets you remember from childhood: the paddle with the rubber ball attached, the cup with the wooden ball and string.

China dolls, of course, and ventriloquist dummies. Tinker Toys, Lincoln Logs, Erector Sets, and the inevitable jack-in-the-Box.

You step through the door, and you're in another world. The owner is predictably old and a bit shabby, a little baggy at the joints.

That special silence—broken only by footsteps on the wooden floor or the subdued voices of the staff and customers—the slightly musty odor, the occasional ring of an honest-to-god cash register: they all transport you to another time.

I wandered to the back, where I found a bin filled with Nerf balls—the kind with the tough, shiny skin. I pawed through them until I found one exactly the right size.

The shop sat at the bottom of a small rise, and as I came out the front door I saw a group of pre-teens on skateboards speed down the hill, just as they might have used it for sledding back east. One of them came barreling along the outer edge of the sidewalk—not eight feet from where that little boy was sitting.

I scooped the kid up, out of harm's way, and turned to present him to his grateful mother.

She swung her shopping bag at me.

This kind of thing happens to me all the time. People don't necessarily understand when you do them a favor.

"Put him down!"

I handed the kid to her.

"That was a close call, ma'am. He almost got hit by that skateboarder."

She looked around. Just my luck, there wasn't a skateboarder in sight. She narrowed her eyes and glared.

"I see," she said.

These situations can be delicate. I smiled graciously.

"Just don't let it happen again," I said.

"Yeah," she said, and lowered her eyebrows at me. "I won't."

She hurried away.

Traveling Angel can be a thankless job.

Julie and Tim were back in Tim's little sports car by then, speeding along the Pacific Coast Highway. The sunset was almost gone, and there was a heaviness in the air that hinted at rain.

Julie stared straight ahead, hoping she could avoid conversation until they reached William's party. Tim's silence was accusation enough; she didn't need words.

Tim took a deep breath through his nose, and she knew it was coming. He snorted in frustration.

"A broken heel."

"I'm sorry."

"By the time we get to your house and back again..."

"I should have brought some spare shoes, or... Sorry."

I took a detour at the edge of town, for a final visit to the new aquarium. The landscaping wasn't in yet, and there were only a handful of exhibits, but it was open to the public.

I paid the entrance fee and went through to the deck overlooking the main tank: a large circular pool, half in the ocean, half on land.

They had added a sign over the deck since my last visit:

The William Hogan Dolphin Observatory

I was surprised by how small the crowd was. This was the big day. I wandered over to the railing and contemplated the water.

The first stars sparkled through the darkening sky. There were thunderclouds on the horizon, and a warm but weighty breeze from the sea. A young docent led her charges toward me, her hair and slacks pulled landward by the wind. I took a deep breath of the sea air, and watched the waves on the surface of the tank.

The docent was in the middle of her memorized lines. Why do they always inject that tone of affection and amusement into every phrase?

"...and fresh sea water," she said, "is constantly pumped in from the bottom as the old water flows out. This facility was specifically designed to accommodate an extremely rare species of dolphin. In fact, the two moving in tonight are the only pair in captivity."

She was right, of course.

I tossed my gift into the water, and resumed my journey to William's party.

My friend William stood in the only place I've ever seen him happy—at home in his kitchen. He was dressed for the party, but was wearing an apron instead of his evening jacket.

Pots and pans covered his cooking island. They gave off hissing and boiling and simmering sounds, and scents of garlic and butter and onion and celery and spices I wouldn't know the name of.

He hummed to himself, tasting and chopping and adjusting the heat under this pot, stirring this one, adding a spice to that one.

I stood in the doorway for a moment, enjoying his bliss, before announcing myself.

"William."

He looked up and beamed.

"Dudley!"

Sometimes in my line of work you need an alias.

6

PART OF THE ECO-MAFIA

I returned his smile.

"How are you, William?"

"I'm so glad you came. Stay here in the kitchen with me—away from the rampant networkers. I hate parties. I don't know why I give so many."

"It gives you an excuse to cook."

I lifted the top of the nearest pot—a garlic cream sauce. I picked up a spoon and sampled it. Nobody cooks like William.

He reached for a wedge of cheese, then grimaced.

"This isn't Brie." He glanced up at me and the grimace vanished. "You know that big deal I was telling you about?"

He looked over his shoulder at Nick, who was working behind him.

"Nick! This is Camembert!"

William's sister, Betty, slipped through the door and gave me a nervous glance. But I wanted to keep William on the subject.

"You mean the pipeline?"

"Wobbling, Nick," he said, "wobbling."

I tried again.

"This big deal. It's the pipeline?"

He grinned at me. "Yes—the pipeline. We sign it tonight. Five years negotiating..."

Betty reached for the spoon in my hand.

"Do I get a taste too?"

William snatched the spoon away and handed her a clean one.

"Where's that son of yours?"

Nick spoke up from behind him.

"He'll be here. He's a—"

"A good kid, I know. I'd prefer a *punctual* kid. Which reminds me—when is that clock going to be fixed?"

Nick didn't respond.

Betty smacked her lips. "Delicious, as always. How should I know? He's staying with you."

"He was supposed to be here at seven. I'll give him till eight, but if he's one second later—"

She laughed. "Would you like me to stand in with the guests—"

"—just one second!"

"—so you can slave away in the kitchen?"

He gave her a grim smile.

"If you see Tim out there, tell him to keep his girlfriend out of the study. There's something in there I don't want her to see."

Nick followed her out to answer the doorbell, and for a few minutes William tended to his creations in silence. I let him, waiting for him to continue on his own. Finally he did.

"Dudley..."

I smiled.

"Don't worry. Tim will be here by eight."

"Do you have to leave tomorrow?"

"I'm afraid I do."

William sighed then. It was very touching.

"I'll miss your bizarre point of view. I have a gift for you. Sort of a combination going-away present and thank-you. If it weren't for you these last few months..."

A gift. I could see it coming.

"I'd rather you didn't give me anything, William."

"I expect to do quite well—actually *very* well—on this pipeline, and I'd like give you a little piece of the deal, so when the profit comes in—"

"That pipeline, William. It's not such a good idea."

"There you go again, with that—that intolerable moral squint. I'm trying to do you a favor."

"If you really want to do something for me, just remember to trust me if things get a little bumpy."

Talk about timing.

At just that moment, Nick came bustling in with Tim and Julie in tow.

Tim looked a bit nervous, the way any kid might, caught breaking the rules. Julie, on the other hand, was completely out of her element in William's kitchen. She was clearly timid and clearly frightened.

William, though, was still reacting to my last remark.

"A little bumpy? What do you mean?"

Tim came right to the point.

"Sorry we're late, Uncle William."

This got William's attention. He sputtered, then narrowed his eyes.

"The guests are already arriving. What time is it, anyway?"

His question was directed at me, and I consulted my watch. It was two minutes after eight. They were screwed.

Then I consulted the panic in Julie's eyes.

"It's seven fifty-five," I lied.

Julie shot me a puzzled look.

I winked.

William growled at the young couple. "You two just made it

under the wire. Go on, don't push your luck, get in there and start greeting people."

William had transformed his living room and deck with miniature white lights wrapped around the railings and the plants. A pianist played jazz standards in the corner, next to the Christmas tree. The room buzzed with conversations. The aroma from the kitchen promised an incredible meal to come.

On the deck, the mayor sipped a cocktail with a member of the town council. She was not happy.

The councilman lifted a casual hand to the back of his head and made a small adjustment to his toupee. "We're going through with this?"

The mayor rolled her eyes.

"A deal's a deal," she said. "But believe me, if I'd had any idea how much resistance there would be to that pipeline..."

"Maybe he won't produce the dolphins after all."

She shook her head.

"In our dreams. William never fails."

I passed Julie and Tim just as the roaming photographer snapped their picture.

Celia, a regular at William's parties, wore a long flowery thing with tassels. She gushed over Julie.

"You're an artist?" she said.

Julie blushed.

"Maybe," she said, "someday."

Celia popped a second hors d'oeuvre in her mouth and kept right on talking. There was plenty of room for both.

"Are you studying at the institute?" she asked, "I could introduce you to some very helpful people."

"I'm applying for the fall."

Tim spoke up.

"Actually, she may be going to UCLA with me."

Celia wiped her mouth.

"I'll introduce you to the director; he's right over there."

She elbowed her way through the crowd.

Julie turned to Tim.

"I wish you wouldn't tell people I'm an artist," she said. "It embarrasses me."

"You're too shy. I don't want people to think I'm engaged to a nobody."

Outside, William joined the mayor. His red top was spinning nicely in the back of his head, but he was nervous anyway.

"Ready for the show?" he asked.

She nodded.

He guided her to a pair of telescopes on tripods at the corner of the deck. He motioned her toward one, and peered through the other himself.

"There they come now."

In the distance, over the aquarium, a helicopter approached. A pair of slings underneath held the dolphins.

As the mayor watched through a telescope, William signaled Nick.

"The contract?"

"It's in the study."

He felt the red top wobble slightly on its axis.

"It's supposed to be here, Nick—and bring my lucky pen."

Nick rushed off.

The mayor seemed puzzled.

"They're trying to wave the helicopter off."

William swung his telescope downward. She was right. The

aquarium staff were standing on the deck, waving their arms wildly and shouting.

His top began a serious wobble.

The mayor squinted into her telescope.

"It's overflowing."

William pointed his telescope toward the edge of the aquarium, where water poured over the edge into the sea.

Something had blocked the overflow tube.

Nick appeared with the contracts and the lucky pen. William grabbed them and waved wildly at the helicopter.

"No! Go back! Don't let them..." His voice trailed off in something like a whine.

The dolphins hit the water, circled the aquarium twice, then went deep. A moment later they broke the surface and soared—high, clean, and free—in a perfect arc, over the edge and into the sea beyond.

William sank into a nearby chair, his face in his hands.

The mayor straightened up and looked at him.

"William..."

"What?"

"Your pen. It's..."

He opened his eyes to see ink dripping on the contracts in his lap. His pen was still in his hand. He lowered it from his face to look at it. His fingers were wet with ink.

His red top, now on its side, rotated slowly to a complete stop.

Bedrooms are full of memories. People used to be born in bedrooms. Some still are. Most of us are conceived in bedrooms —most of you, anyway. We sleep in bedrooms, dream in bedrooms, and a great many of us die in a bedroom.

I was young man—handsome, smart, and full of myself. I already had a little goatee, and I had just begun to learn my trade. With Charlie's guidance, I was getting to be pretty good, too.

I came back from a particularly successful job that night, well past midnight. I eased the kitchen door open, lifting it by the knob a little so it wouldn't squeak, and eased it shut again behind me. I didn't notice the sour smell of age and sickness in the house. It had been that way too long.

There were still dishes in the sink from morning, but I didn't want to risk the noise. I slipped into the living room and down the hall, the noble half of me hoping that Charlie was asleep.

As I passed his room, I saw the lamp on his night stand, throwing a small pool of light around a water glass smudged with fingerprints in a jumble of pill bottles and used tissues.

It was hot. Stifling.

I waited for a moment in the doorway, listening to his ragged breathing, then tip-toed across the room to turn off the light.

"Pup?"

His voice was hoarse.

I paused and turned.

"How you feeling, Charlie?"

"How'd it go?"

I sat on the edge of the bed.

"You'll love this one, Charlie."

"Tell me, Pup."

That was what I wanted to hear. I dived into my story.

"The granddaughter invited me onto the boat," I said. "When I got a chance to talk to the old man, the guy in charge, all I did was listen—just like you told me."

Charlie gave a raw chuckle.

"You've got the touch, all right."

"The first thing you know, he changed his mind. It was incredible."

"And the son—the greedy one?"

"He was furious. But his wife was on my side, so while they argued I slipped into the water!"

"Wasn't that dangerous? How far out were you?"

"Dangerous? I'd left some clothes by the private beach. I just changed back into a dolph..." I stopped myself. "I mean—it wasn't that far, Charlie."

"That dolphin nonsense, again. I'm sorry I ever played that game with you."

"Let me take you down to the sea, put you in the water. It might help."

"You can't live in fantasies, Pup."

"You just don't remember, because of the virus."

"It isn't healthy."

"There's got to be a cure, Charlie, a way for you to go back."

"Stop it! I'm too old and too sick to be worrying about your sanity."

"Sorry."

"Just promise me you'll follow your vocation. Be a Traveling Angel, Pup, like Dudley in that movie. That's what you're good at, what they need."

I patted his hand.

"Of course."

Charlie closed his eyes, but his hoarse whisper continued.

"I couldn't, because of my leg. But *you* can. You're young—and strong."

I shivered.

"Sure, Charlie."

"Promise you won't let anything—*anything*—stand in your way."

"I promise."

His breath began to rattle.

I honestly didn't see it coming.

What did I know? I was twenty-four years old.

"Is this some underground radical thing?"

William and I were in his study. His face was beet red.

"Are you part of the eco-Mafia or something?"

I was trying to get him to see the bright side of things.

"William," I said, "please"

He was between me and the door.

"No," He raged. "I want to know. 'Cause if you're going to kidnap me or something, and hold me until they—they release a blue whale—"

"I can absolutely, one hundred percent, explain everything," I said.

"—I'd kind of like to know in time to PACK!"

I managed to get the table between us.

"It was for your own good, William."

"Because I had really—I know you'll think this is a scream— I'd really come to think of you as a friend—"

If I could just keep him circling the desk...

"Just listen, William."

He was really angry. That vase he was brandishing was his favorite.

"You know what I'm going to do, Dudley?—that's great, 'for my own good'—because you'll be kind of interested in this—"

"Calm down, just calm—"

"I'm going to call the police, and I'm going to have you arrested for, for—it doesn't matter, my lawyers will figure something out."

"We're just going to talk it out, just... please, William..."

He was becoming irrational.

"And I'm going to have you—no, I really don't feel like talking about this, because in three seconds I'll be foaming at the mouth—"

"—just talk it out, William. And when you understand, believe me, you'll be so embarrassed about this scene. You're going to beg my—"

He was clearly in no shape to absorb what I had to say. I decided it was best for him to process his feelings alone for a while.

The vase shattered against the door frame as I ducked out.

I probably shouldn't have told him it was me.

7

CLARENCE ODSBODY

The truth is, that fight with William shook me up.

After I was sure he wasn't going to follow me, I took refuge in the kitchen. He had joined his guests, so the table was no place for me.

Nick gave me something to eat, then left me to serve the others.

I sat there alone, going over it all, again and again.

Why couldn't it turn out right for once? It wasn't as though I were doing it for myself. I never got a penny. Did Albert Schweitzer have this kind of problem?

Nick had a little television on the counter. He'd been watching an old movie—*It's a Wonderful Life*. You know the one. George Bailey—Jimmy Stewart—jumps into a river to save Clarence Odsbody, his guardian angel. Only Clarence has actually jumped in so that George will save him, instead of committing suicide.

While they're drying off, George asks Clarence where his wings are, and Clarence says he needs George's help to earn them.

"Sure," George says. "Sure. How?"

And Clarence—Odsbody—the angel, says "By letting me help you."

Yeah.

~

I slipped out of the house.

The wind had picked up, and it was a lot cooler than it had been. I was wondering whether to take the streets home or walk the beach back. I thought of just heading for the bus station— leaving right then, instead of the next day. I had all my money on me. I could stop by, pay off Kels.

I noticed him before he stepped forward—just a figure, standing silently in the dark, waiting. Maybe I gave some sign that I had seen him. Anyway, he stepped into the light, and then stopped again, as though he were offering himself for my inspection.

It was a homeless kid.

He was maybe twenty years old, if that. He had a few days' growth on his face, and some rags wrapped around his hands. But mostly it was his eyes. They just looked tired. Unbelievably, excruciatingly tired.

The wind whipped between us, tearing at the palm branches over our heads. I could smell the rain coming.

Finally I spoke.

"Do you need something?"

A trace of a smile crossed his lips. He still had a sense of humor.

"A dollar? I haven't eaten in a week."

"A week?"

I was just making conversation. I had already reached for my pocket. But he looked embarrassed.

"Well, not since breakfast."

I began to peel off some bills.

"You have a place to stay tonight?"

He leaned back a little, and a cautious tone came into his voice.

"Why?"

Something broke inside me. I can't explain it, except to say that what I did next was completely and utterly selfish.

I took my entire money roll, and shoved it at the kid.

"Here. Get yourself a bed tonight. It'll do wonders for your perspective."

He took it, but he was still eyeing me, suspicious.

"You sure?" he asked.

"The Seaside Bar and Grill, on Pier Street. It has a shower out back. Ask for Kelsey, he'll let you clean up."

He was still waiting for the catch. He shivered. I pulled off my jacket and thrust that at him as well.

"You might as well be warm on your way there."

"Won't you be cold?"

I realized I had made a decision. I laughed.

"Not where I'm going."

The music and voices from William's party drifted after me as I walked toward the water. I pulled off my tie and tossed it over my shoulder, toward the little white lights on his deck. My decision had given my mood a lift, and on a sudden impulse I sat down in the sand and pulled my shoes and socks off.

I massaged my feet for a couple of minutes and watched the

sky. The cloud cover was low enough to reflect the lights from town.

It was going to rain, all right.

I could hear the breakers clearly now.

I got up and continued walking, feeling the sand, cold, between my toes. How long had it been since I'd felt that? Not since Charlie had...

Good old Charlie.

I was letting him down. I knew that. But I really needed this. I'd earned it—ten times over, or more. All those people, all needing so much help, for all those years.

"I wasn't any good at it, Charlie, that's the point."

I said it out loud, to the sky or the sea. "How many people do you think I actually, really helped? It would be different if I were any good."

I stopped and looked back at the party. I couldn't hear the music anymore, just the breakers and the wind. I was halfway to the sea—the pounding, wine-dark sea. A drop of rain hit the lens of my fake glasses. I pulled them off and flung them out on the sand.

I trudged toward the water again, unbuttoning my shirt.

"You've got to understand, Charlie. I have to do this, before it's too late. Look what happened to you. I want to hear it again. I have to hear it again. Just one more time, that's all."

I was facing the waves. I tossed the shirt aside.

"I'll come back, Charlie. I promise."

I pulled off my pants.

"This doesn't have to be forever."

I stepped out of my shorts, naked, wrinkled and potbellied. The rain was steady now, and comforting on my old skin.

"I'll come back, Charlie, and I'll be better at it because I did this. You'll see."

I knew it was a lie, but I said it anyway.

Then, with an effort of will, I focused on the surf. To my surprise, the sea was still there. She'd never gone away. She'd just been waiting, patiently, for my return. I let the air out of my lungs, and smiled.

"Honey," I mumbled, "I'm home!"

And I strode into the waves.

P icture this:
     Driving rain, as far as the eye can see. Black clouds tinged with light.

The crash of the waves, the taste of salt in your throat. An endless, hopeless aching in your lungs.

I made it pretty far out, but I just couldn't change. It was the first time I'd tried in—oh, in years and years—and it was the first time I couldn't do it. I kept trying, but it wasn't going to happen. I began to realize how old I was. How tired I was getting.

I could feel it calling to me, pulling me down—back into the thick green spaces, back among the fish and the coral and the sounds. Only I couldn't hear them anymore. It didn't feel like home, this time. I was confused, caught between my yearning for those very reaches and my fear of them.

I remembered a nine-year-old, surprised to find that water was suddenly his enemy.

I panicked.

Then I was struggling frantically, the urgency in my lungs driving me—every muscle, every sinew straining for the sand, for the safe and solid land. I fastened on it with my mind, and tried to drag it toward me.

But I was disoriented. And, after a time, I had to admit it. For all I knew, I was headed out to sea.

I tried to conserve my energy, then, to watch for some hint of land light, or a ship.

I drifted for hours.

The water was so cold.

Finally I was gasping and choking and swallowing water. I had nothing left in me, and was thinking of just giving up, of letting myself sink, slowly, into that endless deep, when I heard it.

Funny that it should have been a sound—that I found my way by ear, though I was stuck in a human body.

I heard the breakers, crashing on the sand. I managed to paddle blindly toward them. I picked up speed. My head was out of the water, and I was moving again, breathing.

I began to relax.

Then I felt myself lifted upward. I looked over my shoulder. There was an enormous wall of water, coming right toward me.

I screamed as it hit.

It hurled me toward shore, tumbling this way and that, with sand in my mouth and foam in my eyes. It threw me against the bottom and spun me around, filling my throat with brine and hurting my ears, and just when I thought it was going to kill me, it flung me onto the beach.

The water drained away from the wet sand in front of my

eyes, and I lay there, naked, shivering with the cold and the shock and the fear.

After the longest time, I managed to turn my head so I could see the beach by the light of the storm, stretching out forever...

THE GOLDEN MERMAID

8

GET ONE OF ALFRED'S

Restaurants are almost as important as bedrooms. The world needs a place to sit and eat and drink and talk. A place where you can smell the coffee brewing, where you can see familiar faces, where you can take a break from work and worries and deadlines.

The Golden Mermaid—the restaurant in the drawing on William's writing table—had been that kind of place once, but it had come on hard times. The building needed paint. The asphalt in the parking lot needed patching. The weeds growing through the cracks in the asphalt needed to be pulled.

Even the morning light and the newly washed air after a storm couldn't make the place look inviting.

Ann tripped over a particularly large clump of weeds.

She pitched forward, and only managed to avoid falling flat on her face by a particularly quick combination of twist and muscle, which pulled something in her back and sent simultaneous shots of pain down her leg and up to her shoulder.

She stood perfectly still for a moment, breathing deeply while the pain subsided, then straightened herself.

"Shit," she said, and then, "Alfred!"

Alfred had just disappeared through the front door of the Golden Mermaid.

Ann took a step, experimentally.

Everything seemed to be working. She'd just have a dull ache for a couple of weeks. She strode briskly toward the restaurant for a few steps, stopped, reassessed the ache, and cut back to a gentle stroll.

The man was god damn infuriating. For months he had worked, week in and week out, without ever complaining.

Hardly ever, anyway.

She couldn't count the number of times she'd had to ask him to wait a week for a paycheck. Or two weeks. Now, all of a sudden, he had to be paid. Just when the bank was getting tough, just when her vendors were refusing credit.

He had no sense of timing.

She jerked the door open.

"Alfred! Ouch! Alfred! You can't just walk out. I need two weeks' notice!"

Alfred had disappeared into the kitchen. He answered her from behind the swinging door.

"I quit two weeks ago! And two weeks before that!"

"I didn't think you were serious."

"Just think of all the money you'll save—I won't be eating all the profits."

How petty.

"Is that what you're mad about?"

Alfred came back through the door, brandishing an enormous kitchen knife with its tip bent at a forty-five degree angle.

He waved it under her nose.

"You don't pay me. You hound me to death. You use my best knife for a screwdriver. Just *try* slicing a tomato with that."

He slammed the knife on the counter.

"No more notices. Call me when your cash flow improves."

And he was gone, without even giving her the satisfaction of the last word.

The front door slammed behind him, and his half-dead pickup ground and clattered its way up the drive to the highway. Ann listened, thinking of all the things she'd like to tell him, then turned her attention to Julie, who was putting out the place settings for breakfast.

Another set of problems to be managed.

"There you are. When did you get home last night?"

"We were a little late, Mom. I need to talk to you."

"And I need to talk to you. Have you written the Art Institute, yet?"

"Sorry, I'll do it today. Mom, at the party last night—"

"It's no good just giving up, you know."

"I saw some plans, Mom. This awful pipe thing, coming right across our beach."

Damn William Hogan.

"He promised not to tell you."

"Then you know?"

This was not the morning she had planned.

"Don't worry about this, honey. Just concentrate on moving forward. Breaking free, that's the important thing. Breaking free."

"Yes, Mom."

Ann picked up a booster seat and carried it to the storage closet.

"Have you redone your portfolio, at least?"

"I will. Did you look at the books?"

"No. And I don't want to hear the bad news this morning."

She opened the closet door.

"What a week. First the institute rejects you, then the loan falls through, then Alfred quits..."

Her eyes floated over the contents of the closet: stacks of paper goods, a broken-down vacuum cleaner, jugs of various cleaning solutions, an aging mop bucket... me...

It will all make sense in a moment.

She found an empty spot on a case of toilet paper for the toddler seat. She plunked it down, and closed the door.

"Believe me, honey, I couldn't handle one more surprise."

She took two steps toward Julie before it hit her.

There was something about that closet. The image that had just flitted through her brain couldn't be right. Could it? She let it flit again. No. It couldn't. Possibly. Could it?

"Mom?"

Julie was staring at her. She must have been standing there, catatonic, for long enough to alarm the poor child.

She spun around and yanked the door open.

Just as she thought. There was nothing in the closet but paper goods, cleaning supplies—

And a naked man.

I smiled.

Ann slammed the door to the closet, then jammed a chair under the knob.

"Julie! Come here, quick!"

A voice called through the door.

"You're absolutely right to do that, ma'am."

Julie came running.

"What's wrong? Are you all right?"

"It's perfectly appropriate," the voice said, "given the circumstances."

Ann leaned against the door.

"Call the police, honey. No! Hold this against the door. I'll call the police."

"Perfectly appropriate," it said.

"What's the matter, Mom?"

"This is a little embarrassing for me, too," it said.

"There's a man in there."

"May I make a suggestion?" the voice asked. "You might want to put a chair up against the door, or lock it if you have a key."

Julie was finally getting the idea. She pulled her eyes back from the closet.

"Who?"

"I don't know. He's wearing a mop."

The bizarre image floated through her brain again: the naked man, the strategically placed mop-head, the wooden handle jutting upward...

She changed her mind once more.

"No. You call the police. I'll guard the door."

"I understand your position completely," the voice said. "You need to feel safe."

"A mop? Mom, what's he doing in there?"

"Actually, I'm hiding," the voice said. "I can explain everything, but I'd just as soon you left the door closed while I do that. Would that be all right?"

Ann said nothing.

"Ma'am?"

Ann really did want to say something. But nothing occurred to her.

"Are you still there ma'am?"

She searched her brain for just the right phrase.

"We're here," she said.

"I went for a swim last night," the voice said, "and got caught in the storm. I woke up this morning on the beach. My trunks were gone. I was looking for something to wear."

She thought that she and Julie must look like a couple of idiots, standing there, listening to a closet door.

"I heard someone come in, and thought it would be best to stay out of sight."

They stared in silence.

"I'm sure you can appreciate that," the voice said.

They looked at each other.

"Are you still there?" it said.

They looked at the door.

"Who are you?" Julie said.

The voice was silent for a moment.

"Clarence," it finally said. "Clarence Odsbody."

Ann exploded with disbelief.

"Odsbody?"

"I apologize for that, too, ma'am."

For some reason that made Ann laugh. She pulled the chair from under the doorknob.

"Julie. Give me your apron."

Before Julie could untie it, the picture floated through Ann's mind again.

"No!" Ann said.

"Wait," Ann said.

"Get one of Alfred's."

Ann opened the door about three inches and pushed the apron toward me through the crack. It was a relief, after holding that mop in place. I still felt she wasn't quite at ease with the situation, though, so I decided to soothe her.

"I'm afraid I didn't get your name."

I thought maybe she hadn't heard me, and was about to ask again, when she answered.

"Ann."

I stuck my hand through the crack in the door. After a while, she shook it.

"Glad to meet you," I said.

She didn't answer.

I tried to open the door, but it wouldn't budge.

"Ann?"

"Yes?

"I'm ready now."

"Oh! Julie, go out in front. Until I call you."

"Mom, I'm not a—"

"Just do it!"

I heard the front door open and close, then found I could move the closet door. Ann gave a little jump as it swung open, and backed away a step or two. We stared at each other for a while. She was a little heavy, but I could see where Julie got her looks.

"Uh," she said at last. "Well, I—I guess you could use one of Alfred's uniforms."

She waved for me to follow her.

"He's our cook. Or was. He quit this morning. But he only took two uniforms, so there'll be one in the back."

She led me through the swinging metal door to the kitchen.

I was truly grateful. I told her so.

"I can't tell you how much I appreciate this, Ann. You're an exceptional human being."

She shrugged and opened the door to a dingy restroom off the kitchen. She pulled the chain and the single, dirty bulb gave off a feeble light. An old cook's uniform hung on a hook, and a chef's cap sat on the counter, in front of the dusty mirror.

"You'll have to forgive the mess. I'm afraid Alfred just left everything lying around—toothpaste, shaving cream, his razor —the man had no sense of order."

I stepped inside.

"If there's anything I can do for you," I said, "anything at all —all you have to do is ask. I mean that."

"Mom."

It was Julie, in the kitchen. Ann closed the door on me, but I could still hear them.

"I told you to go out front."

"Jim Barnes is out there."

"Good. He can help sort this out."

Julie called, helplessly, after her.

"Mom. Wait. That man—I know him."

Julie was terrified, the poor kid.

Everything seemed to be going wrong at once, and, as far as she could tell, it was mostly her fault. At least she seemed to be in the middle of it all.

No matter how many times she went over the finances, the restaurant still lost money. She couldn't get accepted at the Art Institute. Somehow she had gotten herself all tangled up with Tim.

And now there was Mr. Smith.

She should have recognized his voice while he was still in the closet. That was where she went wrong. If she'd only paid closer attention.

But she hadn't.

And then her mother had sent her out front, and it wasn't until Officer Barnes drove up with his puppy-dog smile and gave her the excuse she needed to go back in that she had the chance to actually glimpse him—wrapped in that stupid apron, and without his glasses—but still the same old man who had been so kind to her and Tim the night before.

The problem was, she really owed him for that. At least she owed him not to get him in trouble, which was most likely what her mother was going to try to do—or do by accident, anyway, without trying. And it was all because she'd been stupid enough not to recognize his voice coming through the door in the first place.

She wanted to stay and say something to him when he came out of the restroom, but she didn't dare.

Instead she followed her mother outside to where Jim Barnes was getting out of his police car, grinning from sideburn to sideburn.

She had to stop her before she said something stupid to the police—even if it was only Officer Barnes—and got poor Mr. Smith into trouble.

By the time she caught up Jim Barnes was already talking, his cap pushed back on his head.

"I saw Alfred up the road. He says he quit."

He was holding a picture in his hand—a Polaroid photograph.

Julie sidled close enough to see the picture. It was of Tim's uncle and Mr. Smith, at the party last night. And Mr. Smith's face was circled with a felt-tip pen.

Her mother scowled. "Yes. The ingrate quit."

At that moment, to Julie's horror, a window slid open behind the policeman, and Mr. Smith's head stuck out. He took one look and ducked back in, slamming the window closed again.

Officer Barnes glanced around in time to see the sill go down.

"Found someone to take his place already?"

Her mother laughed.

"Him? No, he just showed up—"

"—on Tuesday," Julie blurted. "And we hired him as a back-up. But he's—he's better than Alfred. I think that's why Alfred got mad."

God! She was an idiot. Her mother was looking at her like she had lost her mind. She wasn't going to help Mr. Smith at all, and she was going to get herself in trouble, as well.

Officer Barnes held the picture up for them to see.

"Either of you see this man last night, or this morning? The one with the goatee and glasses?"

Julie decided to take a chance.

"It's Mr. Smith, Mom. The one who helped Tim and me at the party."

Her mother squinted at the picture, then back at Julie.

"Helped you," she said. "Really?"

Officer Barnes focused his attention back on Julie.

"Did you see him after the party?"

"No," Julie said. "He was very nice to us, Mom."

The officer handed the picture to her mother.

"Neither one of you?"

Her mother pursed her lips. This was not a good sign. But then their gazes met, and Julie thought there was just a chance.

Please. Just this once.

"Actually..." her mother said.

"...Actually I was at home last night."

Julie wanted to kiss her.

Officer Barnes took the picture back and shrugged.

"Well, I hate to stop for nothing," he said. "This new guy's better than Alfred? Maybe I should meet him."

And he walked into the restaurant.

Her mother gave her a single withering glance, and followed.

There was no doubt about it; she was in deep shit.

When Julie got inside, Officer Barnes was already sitting at the counter.

Her mother tried to discourage him.

"I'm afraid we'll be opening late, with Alfred quitting and all..."

But he just grinned his boyish grin. Mr. Innocence.

"No hurry."

"I really don't know how long it will be..." her mother said.

"I'll start with coffee, then. Smells good."

Julie headed for the kitchen. If she could just warn Mr. Smith, there was still a chance they could... She didn't know what there was a chance they could do. She just wanted to warn him.

"If he's not ready," she said, "I'll fix you something. What would you like?"

Officer Barnes laughed.

"You two haven't had any customers in so long you don't know how to act around one."

The pompous little—

"Well, Officer..." It was Mr. Smith's voice, coming from the kitchen.

Julie's heart stopped. She stepped back from the swinging door.

Mr. Smith's head poked through the serving window, in full view of the officer. Alfred's chef hat was pulled down tightly over his hair. His face looked naked without his glasses and goatee, and he held a spatula in his hand like he'd been cooking all his life. He looked absolutely nothing like the face in the photograph.

He grinned at Officer Barnes.

"What'll you have?"

9

THE POWER THEFT

Later that morning, my dear friend William slammed the door of his Jaguar in the parking lot of the police station. He glared at Sam over the top of the car before continuing their discussion.

No one was listening today.

"I'm not obsessed," William said. "He's a criminal. He pretends to be my friend, and then he ruins my deal..."

Sam let out one of his indulgent little sighs.

"You have more money than you'll ever spend. You know what I'd do?"

Yes. William knew.

"What? Walk away from it?"

"Remember the condo complex?" Sam said. "I was into the oil thing before they could throw the contracts away."

Had everyone turned against him?

The police station was just as he remembered it—filthy blond woodwork, the overheated air stinking of burnt coffee, constant chatter and joking among the staff. It was a wonder any work got done.

If it did.

Chief Oakes sat on the edge of a desk, a Styrofoam cup in his hand, telling a story to a sergeant.

This was going to be so much fun.

William coughed.

The chief continued his story.

William coughed again.

The chief kept right on talking.

William spoke.

"Chief Oakes?"

Oakes glanced up, then grinned at his sergeant.

"I'll tell you the rest later."

He wandered over to the counter.

"Yes?"

"I filed a complaint on a Dudley Smith this morning."

Oakes nodded then turned to scan the room. He called out to an officer in the corner. The kid looked about twelve. He was probably in charge of the case.

"Jim! Come here for a minute."

Jim sauntered over.

Sauntered. Did anyone ever hurry around here?

William tried to get the chief's attention back.

"This man is the worst kind of con artist," he said. "I want him brought to justice quickly, before he can ruin anyone else's life."

Oakes condescended a smile, then turned to the boy wonder.

"Officer Barnes, this is Mr. William Hogan. How's the search for Mr. Smith going?"

He knew it. The twelve-year-old was running the case. The kid grinned his sincere little grin and pulled the picture from his sincere little shirt pocket.

"Nobody's seen him, sir. I've shown this to half the town."

Didn't anyone understand how important this was?

Oakes reached for the picture.

"Let me see that."

William tried to get his attention back.

"I really want to impress upon you just how dangerous this man is..."

He was interrupted by Oakes' delighted laugh.

"This is Smith?" the chief asked.

William tried again.

"He wormed his way into my family," he said. "tried to turn my sister against me..."

But Oakes wasn't listening.

"Bill!" he laughed, "Look at this!"

The sergeant came around his desk and took the photo. His weathered face broke into a wide grin.

William tried again.

"He pretended to be my friend..."

They ignored him.

"Flipper!" Bill said.

Oakes nodded enthusiastically.

They were in their own little world. William gave it another shot.

"We went on camping trips together..."

The sergeant waved down another cop.

"Hey, Ted!"

He held up the photo. Ted joined them. It was getting to be a real party.

The twelve-year-old officer in charge turned to the chief.

"Flipper?" he asked.

William took another, half-hearted, shot.

'We went fishing..." he said.

But the chief was answering the twelve-year-old.

"That's what we called him. It was four, maybe five years ago. His name was..."

He wrinkled his brow, trying to remember.

Ted looked up from the picture.

"Jonathan or something."

"Yeah," Oakes said. "Jonathan. He used to hang around bars, down on Pier Street."

The sergeant was still grinning.

"A real character."

Oakes nodded.

"Heart of gold."

This was hell.

William tried one more time.

"Yes, on the surface, I agree. But underneath it all, deep down, he is really one of the sneakiest, most two-faced..."

No one was listening.

"Old Flipper." Ted shook his head in disbelief. "In a dinner jacket!"

The twelve-year-old was grinning like he understood what was going on.

"Why Flipper?" he asked.

William wanted to cry.

"You don't understand," he said.

"He thought he was a dolphin," Oakes said.

"He'd come to shore to save humanity," said Ted.

"The man is evil," William said.

"He claimed to be a dolphin?"

"Actually, he tried to keep it quiet. How did we find that out?"

"He's an evil man," William said.

"He cut the chain link fence for those demonstrators."

Oakes snapped his fingers.

"The toxic waste dump!"

"I knew it," William moaned. "The eco-Mafia."

Oakes eyes were glazed over. The chief of police was back in the past now—unreachable.

"Yeah," he said, "Things weren't going well for me at home. If it hadn't been for that conversation with Flipper…"

Hell.

Absolute hell.

"I don't believe this," William said. "I'm sure there were other times—"

"What about the power theft?" Ted suggested.

Finally, a ray of hope. William leapt on it, greedily.

"Yes," he said. "What about the power theft?"

Oakes was actually giggling.

"Some old uptight rich guy came in screaming one night—"

"Stealing power," William said, "is not a small thing."

Oakes couldn't go on. Ted continued the story.

"Flipper rigged an extension cord from this guy's house so that some homeless people could use electric blankets on the beach."

William gasped.

"That was Dudley?"

Sam opened his mouth for the first time since they came into the station.

"That was your house, wasn't it, William?"

The chief brought his giggle under control.

10

YOUR OWN PULSE

I took Alfred's place that morning. It was the least I could do.

I worked as a short order cook when I was younger, and that was basically all they needed. It was fun to be in a restaurant again. The smell of natural gas and coffee and hot grease. The sizzle of meat on the grill. The strange almost hypnotic cycle of putting orders on, taking them off, cleaning in between.

Though the truth is, it was mostly just cleaning. I don't think we had three customers all morning.

Young Officer Barnes loved my pancakes, and they weren't even my best recipe—just what I could do with the commercial mix Alfred used.

The place really needed attention.

Ann took over around noon, to give me a break, and I walked up the beach until I found a deserted stretch, just a little beyond where I had washed ashore the night before. It was around a bend from the restaurant, so I had some privacy. There were a lot of large black rocks at one end, and I hung my cook's uniform on one of those.

It felt good to get out of that uniform. Alfred was a size

smaller than me. Two around the midriff. For some reason I felt heavy, like my body weighed a ton.

I waded out into the surf, and lay down, almost gingerly. I was still a little sore from my swim the previous night, but mostly I was cautious. The surf wasn't very big there. I wanted a relatively safe place to try again.

Forty minutes later, I dressed and headed back to the restaurant.

It wasn't like riding a bicycle.

About then something was happening in town that became important later on.

Chief Oakes was sitting in his private office, with his feet on his desk, cradling a phone receiver to his ear, and looking at the picture of me and William at the party. He had decided to take a personal interest in the case.

The phone was ringing on the other end, and the chief was daydreaming about the good old days—specifically about the time I had that little talk with him that saved his marriage. It was that memory that had caused him to look up the old file on me. What he'd found in the file had led to this call.

The ringing stopped, and a voice answered.

"North Hills Psychiatric."

The chief swung his feet off the desk.

"Could you connect me with records, please?"

"Just a moment."

There was a brief pause, followed by another voice.

"North Hills. Records."

"Deborah?"

"Yes?"

"This is Chief Oakes."

"Oh! Hi!"

"Do you remember a patient you had there—a Jonathan Smith?"

"The dolphin guy?"

The chief leaned forward.

"Yeah. The dolphin guy. When was he released?"

Julie ran out to meet me from the restaurant.

She was a lot more confident on her home ground. I thought for a moment she was going to hug me, but she pulled herself to a stop about three feet away, and fell into place beside me. She was carrying a large conch shell.

"Hi," she said, not quite looking at me.

"Hi," I said.

She kicked some sand in the air, but didn't seem inclined to talk.

"Thanks for covering for me with Officer Barnes." I said, "You didn't have to do that."

She examined the shell in detail.

"You helped Tim and me with his uncle. I guess we're even."

We walked a short way in silence.

"What do you have there?"

"A shell. You can hear the ocean in it." She ducked her head. "Sorry, everyone knows that."

I nodded, sagely.

"I used to carry one of those with me all the time," I said. "They're very beautiful, aren't they?"

"It's not really the ocean you hear," she said. "It's only your own pulse."

I laughed.

"Only? We'd all be better off if we spent more time listening to our own pulse, don't you think?"

She ignored that.

"What happened to *your* shell?" she asked.

I did what I could to help them.

I cleaned up that back room and the kitchen, scraping years of grease off the stainless steel.

I put the grill stone to good use, and soon the grill was smooth and even again.

I cooked, and improved the menu considerably—adding fresh fish, for one thing. Why they were only using frozen was beyond me.

I convinced Ann to put up a Christmas tree and helped her decorate it. Julie and I repainted the sign out by the highway.

Also, I joked with the customers, making them feel at home.

By the end of the week we were actually making money. Ann hired a cook, but now we needed two, so I stayed on.

Their house was just off the restaurant parking lot: an aging Cape Cod, overlooking the beach.

After I slept in the restaurant for a couple of nights, Ann let me move into their spare bedroom.

Evenings, after closing, we would sit in front of their fireplace and drink hot cider. The flames would snap and crackle and throw flickering shadows on the walls, and we would talk, mostly about the restaurant at first, but then I'd get them to open up a little.

One night, we were telling stories.

"Your turn now," Julie said. "You promised."

I put my mug down. I love the smell of a good fire. Maybe that was what put me in the mood.

"Okay," I said. "Well... Once upon a time, a very, very long time ago, when the earth was not so old, or so worn, as it is now, there were a group of—hmm. I guess you'd call them overseers—on the planet. They took care of it."

Julie nodded.

"Humans," she said.

"No," I said.

"They weren't?"

"They weren't. They were dolphins."

She puzzled over that for a moment.

"Where were the humans, then?"

"Don't be impatient. I'm coming to that. The planet got on pretty well by itself, back then, so these dolphins, the overseers, they had lots of time on their—their fins. They soared through the thick green ocean spaces, played games, told stories, explored every inch of the planet—"

Julie interrupted again.

"You mean of the sea."

"Did I say of the sea? The whole planet."

"So it was all sea then."

"It had about as much land as it does now. Who's telling this story?"

"How did dolphins explore the land?"

"Very clever. They had one shape for the sea, and another shape for the land."

Julie had completely forgotten about her cider.

"Really?"

"They could change back and forth, any time they wanted. Some of them even liked the land so well that they chose to live there."

"And not go back to the sea at all?"

"Exactly. That was the beginning of the virus."

"The virus?"

"Well, they called it a virus. They really don't know what it is."

I sneaked a look at Ann. She had stopped her knitting. I continued.

"The way it is with dolphins, they draw their life from the sea. The sea is the source of a dolphin's soul."

"And the ones on the land couldn't?"

"Well, if you're a dolphin, you never completely lose touch with the sea. You carry the sea inside you. It's the deepest part of you. It gives you your dreams."

"Nightmares, too?"

"Not sleep dreams. The dreams you live by, the ones you follow—your deepest desires, that tell you who you really are."

Julie's eyes sparkled from the fire. I took a sip of my cider.

"Well," I said, "these dolphins—"

"The ones on the land."

I nodded.

"—They stopped listening. Not all at once, understand. It took—oh, generations. But in the end they became afraid of the sea."

Julie considered this.

"The one inside them, or the real sea?"

"Both. They forgot they were dolphins. They lost their dreams, and they stopped taking care of the world."

"But what about the dolphins in the sea?"

"Oh, they did what they could. They would come to the land, try to help the land dolphins—"

"You mean the humans."

I have to admit, that impressed me.

"Very good! —try to help the *humans* listen to the sea again. But it was dangerous. The humans didn't listen to themselves, so it was hard for them to listen to anyone else."

I leaned forward.

"They began to be afraid, especially of strangers. So when the dolphins came to help, they weren't always welcome. But that wasn't the worst."

"What happened?"

"After a long time, the problem became contagious. That's when they started calling it the virus."

"Contagious?"

"The dolphins who came to shore to help—well, they stopped coming back to the sea."

"They lost their dreams, too?"

"When the sea dolphins realized what was happening, they stopped sending the helpers."

"They just gave up?"

"Well, almost. There was one very young dolphin who still really wanted to try. He thought if he went ashore knowing there was a virus, he might get back alive."

"They let him, didn't they?"

"Not at first. But he was very persistent. So, years and years after any dolphin had managed to return, this young pup got to give it one last try."

"And he figured it out?"

"No one knows."

"*What?*"

"He hasn't come back yet."

She digested that for a moment, then her eyes became mere slits.

"That's it? That's the end?"

I shrugged.

"It's the way it happened."

She flounced back against the couch, almost spilling her mug.

"That stinks," she said.

Ann gave her a warning look, then smiled at me.

"What's your dream, Clarence?"

I thought about lying, but for some reason I didn't.

"Just to go home."

She picked up her knitting again.

"And what's stopping you?" she asked.

"Oh, mostly a—a transportation problem."

Julie stopped pouting just long enough to comment.

"It's a rotten story," she said.

11

ONE OF THOSE DOLPHIN GUYS

"I know why you're here."

It was the next afternoon. Julie and I were side by side, rolling paint on the deck at the restaurant. When I didn't answer, she looked up and scratched her nose with the back of her wrist.

"You've come to help us."

I dipped my roller in the tray, and tried to scrape the excess paint off the outer edges.

"To help you?"

"Yes," she said. "It's just too much of a coincidence. Alfred quits, the institute rejects me, Mom's deal with Mr. Hogan falls through—and then you suddenly show up."

"Your mother had a deal with William?"

Of course.

"Yeah. She was going to let him ruin our beach with this ugly pipe thing. You show up, and, surprise, you can cook, and business gets better..."

I interrupted.

"Do you still see William's nephew?"

"Tim? Yeah. You're just like that angel guy on TV."

"Do you think he'd talk to me without telling his uncle?"

She considered.

"He might. Probably."

"Would you ask him?"

"Sure. The thing is, I've figured it out. You're one of those dolphin guys."

I knew I shouldn't have told her that story.

"I already told you," I said, "we all are."

"I mean the ones that can still change back and forth."

I couldn't answer that.

When I was little, Charlie and I used to sit for hours on the beach, listening to our friends call from the sea. Sometimes we'd swim out to see them, dive down deep with them, even join a party. Dolphin parties are something special—though actually not all that different from William's gatherings.

For a party, you need two things: a place and lots of people.

For dolphins, the place is no problem—the sea is nothing but endless place. You just need a spot that's deep enough, because a dolphin party is shaped pretty much like a big ball, made up of hundreds of dolphins—the party-goers—swimming in and around each other, socializing, interacting, sometimes touching each other—just like William's parties.

And just like a human party, sometimes a couple will pair up and go off together. But that isn't all a dolphin bash is about, any more than it is for humans.

I never got to pair off. I was too young before Charlie. When I went with Charlie, later, he never changed into a dolphin, so neither did I. But we used to have great times.

Later, Charlie was different.

I stood in the kitchen door, looking across the beach and listening to the dolphins. I was probably twelve or fourteen, still skinny and pimply and uncertain.

The sky was overcast, an even gray, and the sea echoed the color, only deeper. The air was still. There must have been a hundred or more out there. I couldn't see them; they were so far out I had to strain to hear them.

"Close the door, Pup."

It was Charlie, standing behind me. I started to protest.

"But Charlie, I want to hear."

He snapped at me.

"I said CLOSE it."

I froze.

Charlie had never snapped at me, all the time we'd been together.

Not once.

It was as though the basic nature of my world had changed in a split second. I couldn't make his words or manner fit anything in my experience, so I just stood there, dumb and motionless.

Charlie gave a little huff of impatience, then limped over and grabbed my arm. He pulled me inside, just roughly enough that it kept me confused, and slammed the door shut himself.

I must have looked terrified, because when he turned back he stiffened, but only for a second, then something melted inside him. He shook his head, let out a low whistle, and took hold of my arm again, gently, like he did when I was first learning to be a human.

"It's the virus, Pup. That's all. I just can't stand to hear them. Go on out, if you want."

I wanted to go out, wanted it very badly, but there he stood, already shorter than me, wearing that stupid apron, ready to give me anything—absolutely anything.

"It's okay, Charlie," I said. "I'd rather be here, with you."

Two days after my little talk with Julie, Tim was sitting with his Uncle William on the deck behind the beach house. He was watching William intently, or trying to. It was difficult, because he was facing into the sun, and because William had his nose buried in the *Wall Street Journal*.

He took another bite of his eggs, another sip of juice, squinted at the top of his uncle's head over the paper, and finally gathered the nerve to speak.

"So, how's business—lately?"

William did not respond.

This posed a problem. If his uncle had heard him, but did not want to be disturbed, it would be suicide to try again. On the other hand, if he really hadn't heard him, then Tim needed not only to try again, but to raise his voice.

Tim took another sip of his juice, watching the motionless *Journal* over the rim of the glass.

The paper stirred.

William looked up.

"What did you say?"

Tim swallowed his juice a little too fast. It made a painful lump all the way down.

"I was just asking, how's business?"

William nodded.

"Fine," he said. "Fine."

He gave a perfunctory smile and returned to his reading.

Tim put his juice glass down.

He contemplated the wall of newsprint between them.

How did he get into these things?

He took a deep breath.

"I've been seeing a lot of Julie."

William's voice came from the other side of the paper.

"What happened to that other girl—Chris, wasn't it?"

Tim swallowed a little more carefully this time.

"She went off to Europe. You know Julie's mother's restaurant?"

"Her restaurant."

"Yeah. It's really a great place, kind of funky. But she doesn't have the money to keep it going."

A long pause.

"It can be a difficult business."

"I was kind of wondering, actually—she might be looking for a partner."

William's eye's appeared over the top of the *Journal*. He folded the paper up methodically, placed it beside his coffee, then turned his full attention to his nephew.

Tim shrugged.

"I thought maybe—maybe you might be interested?"

He reported to me in town that afternoon. We had arranged to meet at a little art gallery. I picked it because the owner is an artist himself, and sometimes exhibits his own paintings, still wet.

I love the smell of oil paint.

One of the paintings in the shop—not by the owner—is of a dolphin, a female, under water. It's a lovely piece of work, every curve, every shadow true. And the subject—well, she was a beauty. I was admiring it when the little bell over the door jangled and Tim came in.

The boy would never have made a successful spy. He stepped in looking over his shoulder, and practically ran into an easel. The way he played with his collar, the way he kept glancing around to see who was looking at him, if I'd been the store clerk, I'd have figured he was there to steal a painting.

Finally he spotted me and sidled over.

I nodded at the artwork.

"Isn't this great?"

Tim scanned the picture.

"Yeah, I guess."

"So what happened?"

"I brought it up, like you said, and he did listen..."

My eyes were still on the painting.

"Good. Excellent. Just look at that. It's so—so erotic. So he's interested?"

"I guess. I don't know. He didn't exactly say so. Erotic?"

"Yeah. It just makes your heart pound to look at her. Look at the way she's twisting her—"

He was staring at me.

I put my hand on his shoulder, and moved him toward the door.

"You'd better go now. We probably shouldn't be seen together. You did just fine, just fine. I'll talk to you again."

"Did you say erotic?"

I pushed him outside.

12
———

KEEP THE MOTOR RUNNING

My work was almost done.

The Golden Mermaid was back on its feet. They had a new menu. The place was cleaner than it had been in years.

The parking lot still needed work, and they could use some more decorating and polishing. They'd have to hire a new cook. But the important thing was they had customers again. All they really needed now was financing.

William would take the bait. I was sure of that. Ann would get a partner, and some much-needed capital. And it would be good for him, as well. He needed another project to replace that misguided pipeline. What would be better for him than a restaurant?

Mazie drove one of the delivery trucks that came to the restaurant. She was blond, in her late thirties, I would guess, with a matter-of-fact air about her that matched her jeans and work boots. We were nearly on the southern end of her route, which started about a hundred and twenty miles north of the restaurant.

She agreed to give me a lift on her return trip one night.

I was all packed.

They'd miss me at first, but they'd adjust. One of the tricky things about my line of work is the people. They get attached to you. It's always hard on them when the time comes to move on. I wish I could do that memory thing that Dudley does in the movie—make them forget me.

I'd picked a good day to leave.

The lunch crowd was the best we'd had in a long time, and there were already plenty of reservations for dinner. It was quarter past four, a slow time in a restaurant, and the place was empty except for Julie and me.

We were taking advantage of the lull to clean up a little, and set the tables for dinner. The afternoon light slanted through the windows, and Julie was humming to herself as she wiped a table.

I had decided I should tell Julie I was leaving, even if I told no one else. But before I could say anything, the front door slammed open and Ann strode in.

She was actually grinning.

She stopped at the first table, put her fist down, and leaned on it, cocky. Her tongue was visibly in her cheek, and her head bobbed up and down as she looked from one of us to the other—like one of those little dogs people put in the back windows of their cars.

She kept this up until we both stopped working and gave her our full attention.

"Well, I just got off the phone with William Hogan," she said, "and have I got news."

Julie dropped her cloth on the table.

"What?"

Ann beamed.

"He's going to *buy* this restaurant."

Julie took a moment to digest this.

"The beach too? And the house?"

"The whole kit'n kaboodle."

"But where will we live?"

"*I* will live anywhere I want. And *you* can stop acting so coy, young lady."

"Coy?"

"To think I had to hear it from Mr. Hogan."

Ann turned to me.

"She's getting married!"

A strange expression crossed Julie's face.

"Oh," she said.

Ann held out her arms.

"Tim's a wonderful boy."

Julie gave me a cryptic glance as she crossed the room and submitted to a hug.

Ann squeezed her, all teary-eyed.

"Mr. Hogan is a big donor to the Art Institute, and to UCLA. You won't have to worry about money anymore. Why didn't you tell me?"

"I don't know—I..." She gulped a little air. "Mom, I—"

"I can't tell you what it means to know you're free of this old greasy spoon. It's such a load off my mind."

For some reason Julie kept staring at me over her mother's shoulder.

"I don't know, I guess it's—it's the kind of thing you only get to tell your mother once."

"Oh, and I've spoiled it for you, by finding out before you could tell me. Forgive me, honey. I'm just a selfish old woman."

Julie patted her on the back, her eyes still on mine.

"You're not. As long as you're happy," she said, "that's the main thing."

~

I never did get a chance to tell Julie I was leaving. Ann didn't leave us alone the whole afternoon, and the evening was just as busy as we had expected.

After closing, Ann had to drive into town, and Julie went to the house to do the bookkeeping.

I hung back, working in the restaurant. I'd left my stuff in the back restroom earlier.

Things don't always go exactly according to plan. You have to leave room for the unexpected solution. The main thing was that they weren't stuck with a failing restaurant.

William had a new hobby.

Julie could marry Tim and go to art school.

I could go with the flow—I was just there to help.

~

After I cleaned everything especially well I put the detailed recipes for the new menu on a clipboard in the kitchen, where they couldn't miss them.

I changed into some street clothes, and left Alfred's uniform hanging where I'd first seen it. The delivery truck pulled up outside, and I hurried, locking up, because I didn't want Julie to come investigating.

It was raining—not a storm, but steadily, enough to get you wet. I had to laugh. It was the first rain since the night I had arrived.

Mazie waved from the truck, looking weary, but glad to have company for the long ride home.

"Come on! Let's get going!"

I ran around the front of the truck and jumped in beside her. The whiff of oil and metal carried a sense of adventure. I could feel the springs through the upholstery.

"Thanks, Mazie."

I had to yell over the engine.

She nodded, and yelled back.

"All set?"

"Yeah."

She backed the truck around, the gears whining a little, and shifted into low. I glanced at the house. The only light on was in the kitchen. Julie, doing the books. It made me remember something.

"Damn. No—wait."

Mazie stopped the truck.

"What is it?"

My goodbye note was still in my pocket.

"Keep the motor running," I yelled.

I jumped out of the cab and ran, as quietly as I could, to the house.

I eased in the front door, and stood still for a moment, letting my eyes adjust to the dark. I decided the mantle was a good place. I slipped across the room, banging a shin on the couch and stifling a little grunt of pain.

I propped the note against a brass Santa Claus, and found my eyes had adjusted better. I had no trouble seeing my way out.

My hand was on the knob when I heard Julie crying.

I kept my hand where it was. Mazie was waiting outside. It was time to move on.

But she kept right on crying.

This is another problem in my line of work. Sometimes leaving is a little difficult for me, as well as for them. You just have to steel yourself, for everyone's good.

I slipped over to the kitchen door, and opened it a crack. There she was, back to me, head down on the bookkeeping, her thin shoulders shaking. I took a deep breath and backed away from the door.

Mazie was writing on her clipboard when I jumped back into the cab. She looked up, and stuffed it down next to her seat.

"All set?"

I took one more glance at the house.

"Let's go."

She jammed it back into first and let the clutch out.

The rain pounded on the windshield.

Remember that scene in *It's a Wonderful Life*? You know, where Clarence, the angel, asks Jimmy Stewart to help him earn his angel's wings, and Jimmy says...

"Sure, sure. How?"

...and Clarence says...

"By letting me help you."

P icture this:
It's nighttime on the highway.
The rain comes down in sheets.
A delivery truck pulls over to the side of the road.

You jump out of the truck.
You pull your bag down, thank Mazie one more time, and stand there, in the rain, as she waves and pulls away.

I was soaked to the skin by the time I'd walked back to the house.

DOLPHIN LESSONS

SOMETHING BETTER

We all have one: an attic, a basement, a closet—a place in the twilight, the recesses of our world, a place that is not quite with us. Somewhere to keep the stuff we no longer need but can't quite let go of, treasures we'd forgotten, memories.

I don't know what changed my mind.

Maybe just wanting to do it right, for a change.

If I was going to really help, I needed to do a little detective work.

I decided to start by talking to Ann the next morning, but I couldn't find her anywhere. The car was in the parking lot, but no one had seen her at the restaurant, and I couldn't find her at the house.

I decided to take a walk down the beach, in case she had done the same. I pulled on a pair of trunks, and was on my way out of the house when I noticed a door standing slightly ajar in the hallway. I peeked in. There was a stairway leading up to the attic.

Someone was moving around up there.

I knew it was Ann as soon as I heard her. And I knew what it meant. She hadn't been up there in ages, except maybe to bring the Christmas stuff down, but now she had sold the place, and was going to have to move. She was trying to decide what to take with her, what to leave in the past.

She thought she might be able to just throw some of it away.

It was a real, old-fashioned attic, something you hardly ever see in California. Someone had laid one-by-twelves across the rafters to form a usable floor. The wind turbine made a regular *squeak-squeak-squeak* over my head, and created a flickering light. Ann was sitting at the far end, on top of an old trunk, sorting her way through a cardboard box. Next to her was a fine old artist's easel, one of those big, stable, wooden ones that usually live in a studio.

Something about it bothered me.

It held a canvas, but the surface was so thickly coated with dust I couldn't make out the painting, in spite of the trouble light hanging over her head. The air was hot, and thick with the scent of dust and dry pine.

She glanced up at me.

I smiled.

"I saw the door open... thought I heard someone up here."

She swayed a little, stretching her back.

"Some of this stuff hasn't been moved since before I was born."

"It's going to be a big change."

She nodded, her eyes wandering over all the boxes and furniture and canvases.

"My mother built this place during the Depression. She got the property for back taxes."

"She sounds like quite a woman."

"A survivor. She had a recipe for cake with no milk or eggs or butter. My father, on the other hand, didn't have a practical bone in his body."

She laughed.

"She called this place—the restaurant and house—my 'legacy.' Built it for me, so I would have a way to make a living. She really loved me, you know."

"You must have loved her, too."

"I did. Actually."

I sat down on an old footstool. It had a needlepoint cushion.

"I was raised by an old codger," I said, "a wonderful character. I think he would have done anything for me. I really miss him."

She put the box down.

"I only stayed because I promised Mother. All these years, I've kept my promise. But I can't have Julie trapped here. She needs something better."

"Something better?" I said.

A small canvas leaned against the foot of the easel. I reached down and picked it up. I was going to let her tell me as much as she would before running down.

"When she was little," Ann said, "I spent hours teaching her to draw. I bought her paint sets, art lessons when we could afford them."

I rubbed the dust from the corner of the canvas with my thumb and held it so it caught a splinter of light that stabbed through a crack in the shingles.

The initials caught me by surprise.

"You did these?"

I had broken the spell. She glanced at the canvas and nodded.

"When I was Julie's age. But there was no money, and Mother needed me to keep the restaurant going."

I picked up another, amazed.

"Did you just give up completely?"

Her voice was quiet.

"Mother needed my help."

I realized what had bothered me.

"Then that's your easel?"

"It was. My father got it at an auction. It made Mother furious—she thought it was a waste of money. I'm giving it to Julie for Christmas. I don't know why I didn't give it to her before."

She reached out and ran her finger along the easel's edge.

"The thing is, I couldn't do it."

"Couldn't...?"

"Oh, maybe once there was a chance—I was quite good, really—but, well, I'd promised Mother. It's too late for me. But Julie's different. She can do it."

I waited. I knew there was more, and this time I was going to keep my mouth shut.

After a while she looked me in the eyes.

"She's got more talent in her little finger than... You think Mother will forgive me for selling the restaurant?"

I chose my words carefully.

"I think the living care a lot more about promises than the dead do."

Ann nodded, satisfied.

"I've kept her dream alive all these years. It's Julie's turn now."

Julie's turn.

14

IT'S JUST A PARTY

I was beginning to get a bigger picture—bigger than just the problems caused by a failing restaurant. But I still didn't know, for sure, what had made Julie cry the night I was going to leave. Teenagers cry. It's not always a big deal, and quite possibly what I had seen was no more than a kid at the end of a bad day.

But I didn't think so.

I talked to Julie the next morning. We were standing on either side of the front door, polishing the glass. She'd used her conch shell to prop the door open. She was quizzing me about dolphins.

"What if one of them—the ones that got trapped on land—used a shell like mine. Do you think they could learn to hear the sea again?"

I chuckled.

"I thought it was just your own pulse."

"I know. I was just wondering."

"Well, it might be a start."

She polished the window thoughtfully.

But her question had struck a chord with me. I began to form the germ of a plan.

"You know what I'd like?" I said.

"What?"

"I'd like to see your private art collection."

"What do you mean?"

"All those pictures you do just for yourself, that you don't show to anyone else...?"

She shrugged.

"I don't have any like that."

I raised my eyebrows. It made me feel like Kels.

"Really?"

She picked at a speck of paint on the glass.

"I don't really have a lot of time to draw, except for the lessons. And when I do have time—I don't know, I just never think of it, I guess."

"Really?" I said, again.

This was getting interesting.

Ann was in the kitchen, precooking French fries.

Potatoes don't cook all that fast, even when they're sliced thin and fried at 360 degrees. So you have to cook them ahead of time, until they're almost done; then, when someone orders them, you pull them out an order at a time and give them their final few minutes in deep fat.

Ann was lowering a load into the deep fryer as I came in. I picked up the kitchen knife with the bent tip, and waved it in front of her.

"You need a new knife."

She glanced at it, then began filling another basket.

"Yeah, I know. Our last cook wasn't very careful."

"I've been thinking about our talk the other day."

"Our talk?"

"In the attic."

"Oh. That."

"I can see why you might resent this place."

"I don't resent it."

"Might want to escape it, then."

She lifted the second basket toward the fryer.

"I'm pretty busy at the moment, Clarence."

"Sorry. It's just that—are you sure Julie feels the same way?"

She stopped, halfway to the fryer, then turned and dropped the basket back on the counter. She wiped her hands on her apron and cocked her head to one side.

"What way?"

"Are you sure Julie wants to escape?"

Her eyes narrowed, and she pressed her lips together tightly before answering.

"Julie doesn't know what she wants."

End of discussion.

I decided to switch the focus.

"You think that's what's going on with Tim, too?"

"What do you mean?"

She was giving off the same warning signs about this one. I plunged ahead anyway.

"Those two don't spend much time together for a young couple in love."

"He was over here just the other day. What are you getting at?"

"It's just that Julie doesn't seem quite as happy as—"

Whatever her limit was, I had exceeded it. She snatched the knife from my hand and slammed it on the counter.

"Look. You've been a great help. I'm very grateful for everything, okay? But I'm Julie's mother, and you're not. So butt out. Got it?"

I backed toward the door.

The next morning, Julie went running on the beach with her mother. She was working up the right approach—and the nerve —to talk seriously.

It was still cool out, and they ran near the water, where the sand formed a firm, wet surface.

She was still reeling from her mother's announcement. She was actually going to sell the restaurant—and their home. She tried to imagine living away from their little cove.

She couldn't do it.

Tim was nice enough. It wasn't that. And she had no illusions—she would probably never do better. It was just that, well, she had never actually said *yes*. She probably would have, sooner or later, but—to lose all this? The restaurant, the beach?

And just when business was so much better.

Just when they had a real chance of making it really successful.

A wave washed up, chilling her bare feet. Her mother moved up the slope a bit, to keep her running shoes dry.

It was a technicality. She understood that. But maybe she wouldn't be feeling so, so... whatever she was feeling, if Tim—or Mr. Hogan, or whoever—if they had only waited until she got a chance to make up her own mind. She had worked so hard, the last couple of years, trying to save the restaurant. She ought to be allowed to say yes or no to her own proposal, after all.

And she really liked running the place, whenever her mom was gone. She was good at it.

Of course, she couldn't stay here forever, she knew that. She had to go to art school, get trained properly. You couldn't make it as an artist these days without training.

But she couldn't understand why her mother would give up the place so easily. There had to be some mistake.

When the wave retreated, her mother moved closer again.

Julie took a deep breath.

"Don't you love the beach in the morning? It's so beautiful here, so full of—of memories."

Ann smiled.

"Mr. Hogan would like to throw a party when we sign the papers on the sale."

"Mom, are you—are you completely sure you want to sell everything?"

"Absolutely. It would be a good time to announce your engagement to Tim."

"What would?"

"The party. You could announce your engagement there."

"I don't know. When is it?"

"Christmas Eve."

Julie frowned.

"Saturday? That's so soon. I need to talk to you about this, Mom. I'm not so sure..."

"Oh, come on, honey. It's just a party. I'm dying for everyone to know."

Another wave washed over Julie's feet. Her mother moved out of the way, again, then back as the wave washed out.

"What do you say, sweetie?"

"Well, I guess they'll know sooner or later."

"Thanks, honey. It'll be the best party you ever had. I promise."

15

THAT'S JUST HOW IT TASTED

I was balancing on the top of a ladder that afternoon, hanging Christmas lights on the roof over the deck, when Julie came outside. She had her conch with her, and was wearing jeans. Ann must have given her the afternoon off.

She squinted up at me, shading her eyes with one hand.

"Isn't this your break?" she asked.

"I finally talked your mother into these, and I wanted to get them up before it's too late."

"But aren't you going swimming?"

Busybody.

"I've given that up for a while. You're not looking very happy."

"I'm going to miss this place."

"Yeah," I said, "Hand me the next string, would you?"

I decided to meddle a little.

"Are you sure you want to leave? Even for art school?"

"It's so important to Mom, you know? And painting—Mom says she spotted it before I could walk. It's the thing I was meant to do, my purpose, my, um... my..."

"Vocation?"

"Yeah. Vocation. That's what she said."

Definitely time to meddle. I set the lights aside and came down the ladder.

"You remember our conversation about the dolphins the other day? About listening to the sea?"

"Yeah."

"You still want to hear it?"

Her eyes measured me before she spoke.

"Sure."

"Well, I've got an idea that you might be one of those who can do it."

"Really?"

"It might take a little work. Would you mind that?"

She smiled a slow, knowing smile.

"Sure. I mean no, I wouldn't mind."

I took the conch out of her hands and turned it over.

"Take this to the beach, and listen to it for twenty minutes. Don't talk to anybody, don't read, don't take a radio. Just listen. Got it?"

She nodded, her eyes grave.

I continued.

"Do that three times before sunset, and once early tomorrow morning. Then come tell me what it was like."

"That's it?"

I considered. Better give it to her straight.

"Except for courage," I said. "It's hard to hear what you're afraid to know. Go on, now."

A few steps away she stopped and looked back, over her shoulder.

"Thanks," she said.

I nodded and watched her wander toward the water. It was clear to me that the kid needed help sorting things out, and this might just do it. On the other hand, who knew? Maybe she could hear the sea like a dolphin—that would be something, too, wouldn't it?

I got back on the top of the ladder, and started stringing where I had left off. Ann came out the door below me, and began clearing a table on the deck. She didn't look up when she spoke, and at first I wasn't sure she was talking to me.

"What was that all about?" she said.

I realized she must have been listening to us through the door.

"Just a little game. Something to amuse her."

She stopped wiping the table, but she still didn't look up.

"I want you to understand," she said. "All I want is for her to be free. It's got to start somewhere."

"I know," I said. "That's exactly how I feel."

Julie was right, of course, about hearing the sound of the waves in a conch shell. It is your own pulse, amplified and bounced back by the shape of the shell. What she didn't know is that your pulse is a wave itself, traveling through your blood, connecting your whole body to the rhythm of your heart.

If you had been a hawk that evening, circling high over the hills behind the restaurant, you would have seen a wonderful sight. Just at sunset, the Christmas lights came on at the restaurant, outlining the roof in red and blue and yellow and green. Behind those lights, the sunset, purple and gold, colored the sky and the sea.

And halfway between the water and the Christmas lights a lovely young woman sat cross-legged in the sand, her ear to a shell, listening, as the rhythms of the sea without and the sea within became one.

I always mix my pancake batter in a large metal pitcher before the place opens for the day. That way, all I have to do is pull it out of the refrigerator, maybe give it a quick stir if it sits too long, and pour the cakes out on the grill.

It's important not to stir it too much, or the pancakes come out heavy and flat.

When Julie came into the kitchen, tying her apron on, I knew she wanted to talk. For one thing, her work was all out front.

I didn't say anything, though. Over the years I've learned that it's best in these situations to let them start the conversation. Otherwise, you can come off like you're prying. No one accepts help from a busybody.

So I kept mixing the batter, and waited for her to begin.

She just stood there.

I mixed some more.

She still stood there.

Finally, I decided to change tactics. A civil hello couldn't hurt.

"Good morning." I said.

She smiled, a little quizzically.

"Good morning."

I kept right on mixing.

She pulled her apron around in front. She seemed to find my mixing fascinating.

Sometimes you have to give things a little push.

"So," I said, "did you listen to your shell?"

She nodded.

I mixed.

She watched.

It's really a matter of judgment in these cases. Everyone's different.

"Did you hear anything?"

"Hear anything?"

"In the shell." I said.

"Oh! In the shell," she said.

"Well, did you?"

"No. Not really."

"Nothing?"

"It was nice—the sunset, and all. I kind of felt my worries going away..."

"I see."

"...but I don't think I *heard* anything—Is that pancake batter?"

"What?"

She pointed to the pitcher.

"Oh," I said. "Yeah."

"Aren't you, you know, over-stirring it?"

I dumped it, and started over.

Julie still stood there, watching me, with her mouth pulled to one side, like she was trying to decide something.

Finally, she decided.

"Clarence, how do you know what's *right* to do?"

"What do you mean, 'right'?"

She chewed on that for a while.

I stirred the pancake batter.

She tried again.

"If you have a big decision to make, and you're pretty sure what's right, actually, but somehow you can't make it feel right? You know what I mean?"

"Let me get this straight," I said. You have a big decision to make, yes?"

"It doesn't have to be my decision, I just mean—you know—decisions in general."

"And you wouldn't care to tell me just what this decision is?"

She shook her head.

I plunged on.

"But you think you already know what the right thing to do is?"

"Yeah, well, I mean, it's sort of obvious... I mean I know it's the only right thing to do and all, but it just doesn't—I can't make it *feel* right. You know?"

"I think so."

I opened the refrigerator to put the batter away. My eyes fell on some grapes I'd stocked for salads.

I looked at her.

"Close your eyes."

"Why?"

"Time for another lesson."

For a second I thought she was going to argue, but then she closed them, and stood there, waiting.

I pulled a grape off its stem and touched it to her lips.

"Taste this."

She chewed, thoughtfully.

"A grape. So?"

"Close your eyes. Is it good?"

"Sure."

"Okay. Now keep those eyes closed."

I took out another grape, and reached over by the grill for the salt shaker. The grape was damp, so the salt stuck real good. I really poured it on.

I put it to her lips.

"Now try this."

She spat it out in her hand.

"Ech! That was awful."

I raised my eyebrows in amazement.

"How do you know?"

She stopped wiping her mouth and gawked at me.

"What do you mean?"

"How did you figure out which taste was good and which was bad?"

"I... I just... That's just how it tasted."

"But how did you *know* that?"

"It either tastes good or it doesn't, that's all."

"And you can just tell that, without any special tricks or techniques or...?"

"Duh. I mean—sorry, but...?"

"What if you were supposed to love salted grapes?"

"*Supposed* to?"

"Yeah. Say I'd been planning this moment since you were born, looking forward to how much you'd love salted grapes?"

"You were?"

"What if I was?"

"Well, I suppose I could give them a second chance."

I salted another one and handed it to her. She did her best to hide her distaste.

"Well?" I asked.

"It's not as bad as the first time. I might learn to like them. Maybe."

"Good. Very open-minded. I'll fix you a big plate of them for breakfast."

Her eyes got wider.

"No. I mean, that's okay. Actually, I—I don't think I like them that much. Actually."

I nodded.

"I think you're a very wise girl. Now get to your work, so I can do mine."

16

DANNY GIVE IT TO ME

That afternoon Jim Barnes—the young officer I met my first morning at the Golden Mermaid restaurant—walked down the main street in town.

I was in an art gallery on that same street, as a matter of fact, admiring a painting.

My young officer friend was not having a good day.

He was hot and sweaty from walking one end of the town to the other. For some reason, Chief Oakes had decided to give top priority to finding this Dudley Smith/Flipper/Jonathan Something character, and the result was that he had to show the guy's picture to almost everyone in town.

He was running out of people to show it to.

Not that he never had a bite. That was the frustrating part. Half the town recognized the picture, and then would proceed to tell him a funny story, or a fond story, or an angry story. The guy had made an impression all right, but no one knew where he was now.

Barnes stopped for a moment to wipe his forehead and consider his next stop. The sidewalk was crammed with shoppers. Even hot weather couldn't slow down the Christmas rush.

His eyes fell on an art gallery two doors down, and he remembered that it had been closed the last time he came by. He reached into his breast pocket and pulled out the Polaroid shot, now a little worse for wear. For the thousandth time he studied the old man with the goatee and glasses, dressed in a dinner jacket.

He wondered what was so special about that guy.

Sure, he was a strange character, but it wasn't like the chief to put top priority on something like this. Not just because some rich guy was upset. From what he could tell, Mr. Hogan didn't have much of a case anyway.

So why did Oakes have him traipsing all over town in the hot sun, when he could be in an air-conditioned squad car, handing out speeding tickets?

When he reached the gallery door he was still looking at the snapshot, and he ran straight into the old man who was coming out the door.

He grabbed the fellow by his shoulders to steady him.

"Pardon me, sir. I'm afraid I wasn't watching..."

But the old guy was grinning up at him.

"Officer Barnes!"

He smiled, trying to think who the man was.

"Oh. Hello!"

There was something familiar about that face.

The man winked at him.

"When are you coming by for some more hot cakes?"

Of course. It was the new cook—out at Ann and Julie's place.

"How are you, Mr.... uh..."

"Clarence, just call me Clarence. Come visit us some morning."

"Sure. Sure, I'll do that."

"I've got an omelet I want you to try."

Clarence pumped his hand and melted into the crowd moving down the sidewalk. Barnes watched him go, a half-smile on his lips. The old guy sure was a character.

He had taken a deep breath, and was about to turn back to the gallery when it caught his eye.

He glanced down at the Polaroid shot, back down the sidewalk, and back at the photo again. Then he began to push his way through the crowd, stuffing the picture into his pocket as he moved.

He went as fast as he dared, wanting to get as close as possible before the old man saw him. He was only about ten feet away when the guy looked back. He saw panic come into the guy's eyes, and he walked a little faster, to close ground.

"Wait a moment, sir, I need to talk—"

But just as he feared, the old man broke into a run.

Great. With the temperature in the nineties. He sprinted after him, swerving through the crowd, which had become a human obstacle course.

The guy was lucky, of course, and had no one in his way. He gained a better lead, then disappeared down an alley. Barnes almost threw his back out managing to thread his way around a middle-aged woman carrying half a dozen bags, a little girl who was walking backwards while eating an ice-cream cone, and a business-man who was trying to pass them both, intent on some emergency of his own.

He put on a burst of speed, and rounded the corner to see his quarry halfway down the alley.

"Stop!" he shouted. "Police!"

The old guy stopped and turned around. Barnes ran toward him, and almost reached him before he fled again. But this time it only took an extra burst of speed, and he pulled the guy to the ground.

It was a moment before he could catch his breath.

The poor old guy was scared to death. He could see it in his eyes, and he felt like a monster because of it. But he had a job to do. Finally, he got the words out.

"It's... It's okay," he said. "You're not in trouble... I just need to... to ask where... where did you get this jacket?"

The old man peered at him with half-comprehending, owlish eyes. His toothless mouth worked soundlessly. After a time, his eyes wandered to the wrinkled formal dinner jacket he was wearing over a chartreuse sweater and a blue sweatshirt, in spite of the relentless heat.

His mouth worked some more.

"Danny," he said.

Officer Barnes tried to ignore the odor that hung about the old guy, even though it was making his eyes water.

"What?"

The old man was impatient now.

"Danny," he insisted. "At the shelter. Danny give it to me."

NICE

A few hours later, William sat in his study in front of some new designs.

He wasn't thinking about the designs, though. He was remembering again—reliving the day his father had visited his boyhood circus.

He and Sam had dragged his dad on a tour of the entire project. They had insisted that he look at every attraction, listen to all their plans, sample their lemonade and cookies. It was unusual for his father to be home, and William wanted very much to impress him while he had the chance.

When the tour was over, Sam wandered off, and William and his father sat at a card table in the field, drinking lemonade. William leaned his chair back, his hands clasped behind his head, doing his impression of a successful businessman—relaxed, confident, even a bit proud.

Inside he was a mess, waiting in dread and hope for his father's pronouncement.

He waited.

His father took a sip of lemonade, his eyes surveying the field.

"It's a great circus, son."

Ecstasy. Vindication. Pride. Joy...

"Mind if I look at your books?"

...Panic.

He tilted his chair back onto all four legs.

"Books?"

His father smiled, a little indulgently.

"Your records," he said. "How much everything cost, how much money you charged. How much you made. I saw you were charging at the gate."

A rising fear.

"That was just to make it, you know, real. We only charged a penny."

His dad nodded.

"How will you pay for the materials?"

Guilt.

"It was stuff from around the house. Mom said it would be all right."

He was disappointed. William could tell.

"It's okay, Will. You're just a kid—"

A touch of shame.

"—But you should think about it. A circus that makes no profit won't be around very long in the real world."

William hung his head.

"I'm sorry, I was just—"

His father interrupted.

"Don't worry about it, son. I said it was okay."

～

Julie stood in the doorway of William's study, waiting for him to speak. She had thought, at first, that he would look up in a moment and see her there, but as time went on she began to wonder.

There was a point at which it became embarrassing to just stand there, and she was tempted to slip away. But what if he looked up, just as she started to leave?

No. She should knock, or say something.

She cleared her throat.

He didn't look up.

She cleared it a little louder.

"Mr. Hogan?"

His head moved a fraction, as if he had suddenly remembered something, and his eyes searched the room until they came to rest on Julie, standing in the doorway.

"Oh. Julie. Hello."

"Do you know where Tim is?"

He waved her into the room.

"Tell me what you think of the new plans. Only be complimentary, because I'm a little sensitive lately. Do you like them?"

She had to walk around next to his chair in order to see what he was talking about. To her dismay, it was a new sketch of the restaurant, except it was no longer called The Golden Mermaid.

It was renamed Willini's, and instead of all the fishnets and mermaids and seashells it was now designed around a circus theme. There were huge awnings over the entrance, crafted to look like circus tents.

Two life-size plaster figures, a roaring lion and a top-hatted ringmaster, flanked the doorway. The building itself was painted with bright yellow stars and circles. It looked completely out of place on the beach and reminded her, somehow, of a fast-food restaurant.

She had a nagging suspicion that all the paint would be thick and glossy.

Mr. Hogan was still waiting for her to comment.

"Yeah," she said vaguely. "They're... nice. Do you know where he is?"

Mr. Hogan still had his eyes on the plans.

"Nice, hmm? Nice. Well that's certainly... Where he is?"

"Tim."

"Oh. He may be up in his room. You think it's... nice?"

Julie did not want to have this conversation.

"Did you design it yourself?" she asked.

Mr. Hogan seemed to be flattered.

"No. Really? Myself. Oh no. I hired the best for this. Everything. Architects, food designers, marketing experts. How do you like the logo?"

"It's all so—so different. From that pipeline thing."

He nodded.

"That's it. Exactly. Completely different. That's the idea."

"The idea?"

Something told her she shouldn't have said that.

"Yes. After that pipeline deal fell through I was furious. I was determined to put it back together. Determined to get revenge. When Tim told me about your mother's restaurant, I wasn't even interested. Then something wonderful happened."

She knew it. This was going to be a long story.

He continued.

"I'd scheduled a little dinner party months ago. I didn't have the energy to cancel it, so I went ahead. At first, I didn't have much enthusiasm about it, so I kept the plans simple. But as I began to cook, something strange began to happen.

"I found myself lost in the task.

"I would be stirring the soup, or kneading the bread, and the whole world seemed to boil down to—to stirring the soup, or kneading the bread. I was completely there. I was at peace with the world. The simplest act—chopping a vegetable—was so intensely beautiful it made me cry."

He glanced up at Julie.

"Did you know that if you put a little bit of onion on your head when you're chopping it, it keeps you from crying?"

"Really?"

He nodded.

"The dinner that evening was incredible. Everything was effortless and perfect. The meal—I served quail in rose-petal sauce—the conversation, the sense of fellowship that filled us all... I'd never had an evening like that.

"And after dinner my friend Sam proposed a toast to me—to me. You know what he said?"

"What?" Julie asked.

"He stood up suddenly, without any announcement or anything, and just waited—until everyone at the table stopped talking, and turned to see what he was going to say.

"He looked straight ahead, not at us. And after a moment of silence, he said:

"'A man must make choices in this life.'

"Then he reached down and picked up his wine glass.

"'With each choice,' he said, 'we fear the loss of what we have not chosen. William has chosen business over his art. But tonight we are witnesses that nothing is lost.'

"Then he lifted his glass toward me, and drank. And everyone there did the same. It was—well, it was incredible. All my life, I'd been searching for something, and now, when I'd finally given up on it, it dropped right into my lap.

"And while they were toasting me, I suddenly remembered something a friend had told me, almost a year before. Actually, you've met him—remember Dudley Smith? He was the man in the kitchen that night you and Tim were almost late for the party?"

"Yes," Julie said. "I remember him."

"Well, we went camping about a year ago, out in the desert. And one night we were just sitting around the campfire, you know, playing bongos and chanting and stuff. And I had cooked dinner over an open fire, and Dudley said to me:

"'Delicious, William. And over a campfire. Absolutely unbelievable.'

"It was cool out, but not cold—perfect, really. I was savoring the scent of the campfire, and watching the flames and the Joshua trees silhouetted against the last light of the evening, and I said:

"'The desert's so peaceful. I'm tempted to move out here—just never go back.'

"And Dudley raised one eyebrow at me, like I'd said something funny.

"'I got to tell you, William,' he said, 'it wouldn't do you any good. You'd be buying this all up, developing it, and selling it off within a year.'

"'I'm not so sure...' I said.

"But Dudley shook his head. Then he pointed to his chest.

"'No. What you need, my friend, is a vacation from whoever or whatever you're trying to satisfy, in here.'"

Julie shifted her weight from one foot to the other. William seemed to have forgotten that she was listening.

"In that moment," William continued. "I knew he was right —had been right all along.

"And that night at the dinner party, after Sam toasted me, I remembered other dinner parties I had given over the years. All the good food, carefully prepared, all the people, warmed and nourished and connected to each other. I realized that I had ignored my real vocation all my life.

"I had spent my life trying to please someone else."

The faraway look faded from his eyes, and he focused on Julie again.

"So I decided to open a restaurant. To provide people with good food, with a warm atmosphere, with evenings like that one."

Julie nodded slowly, trying to take it all in. She glanced again at the plans on the easel.

Under the drawing of the building, below the plaster lion, were sketches of clown suits, designed for the waiters.

She absolutely had to be polite.

"Yes, well, that's—that's wonderful, Mr. Hogan. And you're going to be the cook?"

"Me? No. I'm hiring the best."

"Oh. Well, it's a very nice restaurant. I'm sure you'll... Tim's in his room, you said?"

Mr. Hogan came out of yet another fog.

"Hmm?" he said. "Oh. Yes. He might be. It's upstairs, second door on the right."

William watched Julie leave the study, then turned his attention back to the plans. His eyes wandered over the clown suits, the circus awnings, the plaster figures at the entrance.

"Nice," he mumbled to himself. "Nice."

18

THE SEA INSIDE YOU

Upstairs, Julie wandered down the hall toward Tim's room. Mr. Hogan's house was as quiet as a museum, and the air conditioning brought out little goose bumps on her arms.

Poor Mr. Hogan didn't have a clue. You had to feel sorry for him—you had to.

He actually thought all that circus stuff would make the restaurant better. Of course, she felt bad about it—it had been part of her home for her whole life. Her mother had kept her in a playpen, in a corner of the kitchen, when she was a toddler.

She had worked her butt off, the last couple of years, to help save the place. Of course she hated to see it turned into an—an amusement park. But it wasn't Mr. Hogan's fault. The poor man just didn't know any better.

You had to feel sorry for him.

You had to.

Tim's door was half open. She knocked lightly on the door jamb.

No answer.

"Tim?" she said.

Then louder.

"Tim?"

She pushed the door a little further open, and stuck her head in.

The room was empty—an unmade bed, clothes on the floor, a mess on the dresser—but no sign of Tim.

She turned to leave, but instead froze, motionless, in the doorway.

Something had caught her eye.

She wasn't sure she wanted to know what it was, but she couldn't bring herself to leave, either. She shivered from the air-conditioning, and unconsciously chewed on her upper lip.

Tim wasn't here, and she had no business snooping around his room. She would just go down now, and...

...and never know, for sure...

This was silly. If she really trusted him, she wouldn't be afraid to look.

She turned around, strode directly to Tim's night table, and picked it up.

It was a photograph, of a girl she didn't know, sitting in exactly the same place, exactly the same position, she had been sitting herself, when Tim had so suddenly proposed.

Meanwhile, down in his study, William's thoughts had wandered again. He had started by admiring the plans for his restaurant, but had moved on to a general review of his conversation with Julie, and had ended by remembering, again, the time he went camping with me in the desert.

Since he was very content at the moment, he remembered that trip with great fondness, and then went on to remember other things about me with the same fondness. By the time he was finished, he was even chuckling to himself about the evening I destroyed his pipeline deal.

I wouldn't say he was ready to thank me yet, but he was close to forgiving me.

On a sudden impulse he dialed the phone.

"Hello. This is William Hogan. Let me speak to Chief Oakes, please."

He looked the sketches over as he waited, nodding to himself.

"Chief Oakes here."

"This is William Hogan, Chief."

"Mr. Hogan! I was just going to call you. We've made some progress on Mr. Smith."

"That's what I want to talk about. I want to call off the search."

"Call it off?"

"Yes. I'm dropping all charges. I'll sign anything you need. The man's been hounded long enough."

Oakes' voice was measured.

"Actually, Mr. Hogan, it's a little more complicated than that."

"That's all right, Chief. Just tell me what I have to do. I'll come down to the station, if you want."

"It's not that. It's just—you can drop the charges, Mr. Hogan, but we can't call off the search. There are other people looking for Mr. Smith now."

"Other people?"

"I checked into his background as part of the investigation."

"And?"

"Before you met him, he escaped from a psychiatric hospital."

～

Mazie was just finishing a delivery the next morning. I stood by the back door of the restaurant, checking off the orders on my clipboard, when Julie came around the corner of the building. She was clearly excited by something. She didn't even pause to say good morning.

"I've figured it out," she said. "I have to 'taste' the right thing to do."

Mazie rolled a dolly stacked with boxes of soft-drink syrup by me. I put out a hand to stop her.

"Is that cola?"

She checked it.

"Root beer."

"We only need cola."

She sighed and wheeled it back to the truck.

Julie couldn't stand still.

"I have to taste the right thing. Am I right?"

I raised my eyebrows at her—I was getting good at that.

"What do you think?" I said.

Julie searched my eyes, then laughed.

"I'm right. I know it."

Mazie came back with the delivery form.

"So how do I do it?" Julie asked.

I waved her off.

"Just give me a minute, okay?"

I signed the form, took my copy, and thanked Mazie.

Julie was practically jumping out of her skin.

"How do I taste what's right?"

"Not like that. You have to calm down first."

I steered her over to an open step-ladder I'd been using to clean out the rainspout.

"Sit."

She sat down, and tried to contain herself.

"Now close your eyes, and take a couple deep breaths. Let

them out real slow."

She did.

"Feeling a little calmer?"

"Uh-huh."

"Okay. Now, tell me, where exactly is this problem?"

Her eyes popped open.

"What do you mean?"

"Where do you feel it? In your head? In your back?"

"Oh."

She closed her eyes again.

"It's—it's somewhere in my stomach. I think."

"Okay, in your stomach... now, what does it feel like?"

She giggled.

"This is stupid."

"Fine," I said. "I've got work to do."

"Okay, okay. I'll try."

She concentrated for a moment. "It feels like, like—it's not in my stomach! It's in my throat! Like I can't breathe."

"Like there's no air," I said.

She shook her head violently.

"No. More like I'm holding my breath."

She became very still, and spoke in a whisper.

"Yeah," she said. "Wow."

I bent close to her.

"That feeling, like you're holding your breath, that's a wave, from the sea inside you."

"Really?"

"Really. Now ask the sea—ask it what that wave means."

"Well, I guess it means..."

"No! Don't guess. Ask. Ask all that water behind the wave. And wait. Wait for the answer."

"Okay, okay. Just give me a minute..."

She waited.

After a minute or two, she took in a short, startled breath.

"It's about... I'm suffocating... like someone's holding a pillow over my face, except it's really me, because I'm holding my own... Oh!"

She took a deep breath. When she let it out, her whole body seemed more relaxed.

She opened her eyes, and looked at me, surprised.

"The wave," I said. "That feeling that you can't breathe. It changed, didn't it?"

She moved inward for a moment and then came back.

"How did you know?"

I shook my head.

"What did you hear?"

She considered.

"Do I have to tell you?"

The best thing to do at moments like this is relieve the pressure. When they know they don't have to tell you, they usually do.

"Absolutely not," I said. "The important thing is to welcome whatever the sea tells you—even if you don't do anything about it."

"Welcome it?"

"Be grateful. Thank the sea for telling you. You don't have to do anything about it, but don't stop listening—understand?"

"I think so."

"Of course, you *can* tell someone—if you think it will help."

She thought about it.

"I don't think I want to, right now."

I could handle that.

"Fine," I said. "No problem. I have work to do."

I left her there, lost in her newfound discovery.

The door only slammed because I was in such a hurry to get back to work.

Around noon that same day Officer Jim Barnes stood in the doorway of the Seaside Bar and Grill, trying to catch the eye of a waiter. Business was booming, and each time he tried to flag one down, they shot past him to take an order, or deliver one, or to run to the kitchen.

He was about to give up and come back later when Kels spotted him and ambled over.

He raised his eyebrows.

"Officer?"

Jim Barnes was so relieved he could have hugged him.

"I'm looking for a Danny Albright?"

Kels looked him up and down before responding.

"Danny. He in some kind of trouble?"

"No. Oh!—no. Not at all."

Kels nodded, cautiously.

"Because he's a good kid."

"No. It's nothing like that. I just need to ask him about something."

Kels looked him up and down again, then turned, and bellowed across the room.

"Hey! Danny!"

A good-looking young waiter in the far corner glanced up.

Kels waved him over.

He excused himself from his customers, and navigated his way across the crowded room. When he arrived, he nodded to Officer Barnes, warily.

Barnes nodded back. Everyone here seemed to be afraid of something.

"Danny Albright?" he asked.

"Yes."

"Do you know a man named Barry who lives on the street in town?"

"I know Barry, from the shelter. I volunteer there two nights a week. Is he in some kind of trouble?"

Barnes detected a sense of relief in the young man's voice. He decided to come to the point.

"He's wearing a jacket. He claims he got it from you."

The fellow was suddenly on his guard again.

"A jacket?"

Barnes held up the Polaroid snapshot.

"I'm looking for its owner," he said.

P icture this:
	You're lying flat on your back, staring upward, through the water. Your arms are weightless at your sides. Every sound is magnified by the water on your eardrums. You are cold, and you aren't sure how long you can hold your breath.

Above you, you can see the surface and the light, and every cell in your body aches to reach it, to burst through to the light, to the air.

I stayed under anyway, steeling myself, praying for the change to come.

I felt the pressure build in the back of my head, behind my eyes.

My lungs developed a will of their own, and tried to breathe without my consent. They didn't seem to mind that it would be water, that I would drown. They just wanted to suck something in.

But I fought them. I held my mouth closed tight against

them. I closed my eyes so I wouldn't see the surface, so tempting, so close...

Then my mouth sided with my lungs, and started to open.

I sat up, so fast that I started a wave, and some of the water sloshed over the side of Ann's claw-footed tub and onto the old linoleum floor.

I gulped a huge lung-full of air, managed to get a bit of salt water down my windpipe, and choked.

When I stopped coughing and spitting, I grabbed the box of salt on the edge of the tub and threw it across the room.

THE VIRUS

19

THE STUPID GRAPE

It was lunchtime, for us, that is: about four in the afternoon, when we could count on a lull in business. I fixed Julie and Ann a fruit salad and served it to them at the counter. I hung around, cleaning and straightening, in case they wanted something else.

I figured they deserved to be waited on once in a while. I'd eat later.

They were talking about William's upcoming party.

"...you can call any other friends you want," Ann said. "There isn't time to send out invitations."

Julie seemed to be preoccupied.

"Okay," she said.

Ann continued.

"Just think. By this time next year you'll be away at college, and married. I'm going to miss you."

This brought Julie into focus.

"You know, Mom," she said, "maybe Tim and I should wait a bit."

Ann laughed.

"That's sweet, baby. But you don't need to worry about me."

Right there, I missed a great opportunity to keep my mouth shut.

"Maybe she isn't sure what she wants," I said.

Ann never even glanced in my direction.

"Have you decided who to invite, dear?"

Julie sighed.

"Well, I thought Evelyn, and maybe the Thorndike twins..."

There are moments in your life when you've already overstepped your bounds, when you really ought to save your shots, pack it up for the day, and go home, but you don't. It's not rational; you're quite aware that you're pushing your luck, but you just quite suddenly stop giving a damn.

Maybe it was because Ann froze out my ill-conceived remark, maybe it was because I was sick and tired of watching Julie being pushed around, maybe I'm just sporadically perverse by nature.

Maybe all of the above.

I reached my hand toward Julie's plate.

"May I?" I said.

Ann was still rambling on.

"Oh, I think we should invite the whole family. What about Robert and his sister?"

Julie glanced at me.

"Sure," she said. Then, to her mother, "Yeah, I guess we should ask them."

I took a grape off her plate, then I leaned on the counter, back a way, so I was behind Ann, but looking right at Julie.

I locked eyes with Julie and methodically salted the grape, until every bit of it was covered with white. Then, still holding her gaze, I plopped it into my mouth, and began to chew.

Ann was still jabbering on, about the party.

"I think I'll buy you a new dress for Saturday. You don't get to announce your engagement every day."

Julie understood. And to my surprise she acted on it.

"Mom," she said. "I was at Tim's yesterday, and I went up to his room, and there was picture there, of this other girl—"

Ann saw it coming, and tried to head it off.

"Oh, honey, don't work yourself up over a little thing like that. Just because he has a picture of a friend in his room doesn't mean—"

But Julie—maybe for the first time in her life—interrupted her.

"She was sitting on this rock, Mom—the exact same rock that I was sitting on when Tim proposed, and—

Ann interrupted right back.

"So?"

"Well, it was kind of strange, seeing her sitting there, just exactly—I mean exactly—like I was..."

Ann looked exasperated.

"Who took you to that rock?" she asked.

"But that's not the point..."

"Who?"

Julie sighed.

"Tim."

Ann smiled, triumphant.

"So the mystery is solved. He knew about the spot because he had been there before."

Julie shot me a desperate glance.

"You know what I think?" Ann asked.

I had never seen Julie look so miserable.

"What?" she mumbled.

"I think my little girl is finding out what cold feet feel like. It's perfectly natural."

"But, Mom..."

"You're getting the chance I never had. That makes me so

happy—I can't tell you. But if you're going to swim, you have to jump in, dear."

She moved forward, and gave Julie a hug.

"So you just ignore those cold feet, honey. Besides, it'll be good practice for the wedding."

Julie gave me a helpless look over her mother's shoulder. It reminded me of the day her mother told us about selling the restaurant—the day I had planned to leave.

Maybe I should have.

But there was nothing I could do at the moment. I gave her a sympathetic smile, and shrugged my shoulders, holding up my helpless hands.

That was when I looked past her, and saw Ann, watching me in the mirror at the end of the counter.

I spit the stupid grape into a napkin.

So that's pretty much how it went. There wasn't a whole lot I could do to help Julie, but I couldn't just let things be, either. On the day of the big party I was still trying. Ann had closed the restaurant at eleven so she and Julie could have plenty of time to get ready, which gave me the rest of the day off.

I wasn't exactly invited.

I had set up a beach chair just in back of the restaurant, looking out to sea, and had settled down in a new Hawaiian shirt, a pair of shorts, and a big straw hat to while away the afternoon. Julie had settled down beside me on a blanket, sunbathing. I think she was hoping to improve her tan for the party.

Ann called down to her from the deck above.

"Don't forget the time, Julie. You have to be ready to leave in just two and a half hours."

Julie called back without looking up.

"I haven't forgotten, Mom."

Like I said—I couldn't leave it alone.

"Why all the rush," I asked, "about announcing your engagement?"

I should have waited until I heard Ann go in.

Julie pretended not to understand me.

"All the rush?" she asked.

"Well," I said, "maybe I'm wrong about that. You know, I make assumptions. How long have you known Tim?"

Ann's feet thumped across the deck, and the door slammed behind her.

"Shit," I said.

Julie sat up.

"What's the matter?"

It was no coincidence that two minutes later, on the other side of town, Chief of Police Oakes was being flagged down by Sam, the officer on the desk.

"Chief!" he said, "I got a call—about Flipper."

Oakes crossed the room in two long strides and scooped up the receiver.

"Chief Oakes here."

The woman on the other end of the line spoke in a half-whisper.

"One of your officers, Jim Barnes, showed me a picture—of a man with a goatee?"

"Yes, ma'am. Do you know something about him?"

The door onto the deck had a slight tendency to squeak, so I held it firmly and opened it with a quick, smooth, movement. Once inside, I closed it behind me the same way.

Ann was talking on the phone at the front desk, just as I had feared. If I was right about that, I was probably right about who she was talking to. The wall hid me from her view, but also kept me from hearing her clearly. I crossed the room as quickly and quietly as I could, and slid along the wall until I was just around the corner from her.

There I could hear just fine.

"...and this is confidential, right?" she said. "I mean no one's going to tell him—afterward—who it was who called?"

That was all I needed to know.

20

I DON'T SEE THE DIFFERENCE

I slid back along the wall until I would be out of sight crossing the room, then slipped across and out again. Once I got the door closed behind me I was across the deck and down the stairs in a half-second.

I paused below the deck just long enough to grab Julie's arm and drag her to her feet.

She pulled back a little.

"Hey! What are you doing?"

I marched her toward the water.

"Come on," I said.

She dug in her heels and dragged us to a stop.

"What—Where are we going?"

"It's time for your last lesson."

"Now? I've got to get ready for the party."

I let go of her arm, and took a step closer. I couldn't afford to blow this one.

I lowered my voice, and gave it every ounce of urgency I had.

"I don't have any time left. If you are going to help, you have to do what I tell you—no questions, no argument. Can you do that?"

"But I've got to—"

I cut her off.

"Can you *do* that?"

She searched my eyes for a moment, and gave a quick glance back toward the restaurant.

"Yeah, okay, if it's that important."

I took her arm again, and started walking toward the water.

"Are you in love with Tim?"

"Tim? What's that got to do—"

"I told you, I don't have time to explain. Do you love the boy?"

"I... I don't... It seems to be right for everybody. Like the right thing to do, you know?"

I took a quick look back at the restaurant myself. We had reached the wet sand at the water's edge.

"Okay. Walk out until the water is up to your waist."

She hesitated, then started out into the waves. When she realized I wasn't following, she stopped and turned.

"Aren't you coming in?"

The truth is, I had intended to.

"I can't." I said, "Just keep walking."

A wave washed close enough to touch my feet, and I leapt backwards to avoid it.

I had less time than I'd thought.

"Okay," Julie said. "Now what?"

The water was up to her midriff. I had to shout above the roar of the surf.

"Now, as you go deeper, feel the sea around you becoming one with the sea inside you."

"What?"

"You've got to trust me on this, Julie. You've got to."

"I'll try."

She moved a little further out.

I took another look over my shoulder.

Nothing yet.

I looked back at Julie. She had stopped moving, and was facing shore again.

"Can you feel it?" I called.

She shook her head.

"I don't know."

"Move a little deeper!"

She shook her head again.

"I'm coming out."

She started toward me. I wanted to scream. If I only could have made myself go into the water.

"No!" I shouted. "Go back. This is our last chance."

"What do you mean?"

There was still no activity at the restaurant.

"Back to where you were," I shouted. "Now!"

Julie backed up a few steps.

"Okay, okay."

"You've got to think," I shouted. "No!—Feel! You've got to feel the sea. Feel yourself becoming one with the sea. Feel the water moving over your fins. Feel your—"

"My fins?"

She walked toward me again.

"I can't do this."

I shouted louder.

"Feel your dreams, Julie. What you really want out of life..."

She was out of the water. She was going to walk right past me.

"I'm going to get ready now."

I stepped in front of her to block her way.

"No, Julie, you don't understand. You've got to get in touch.

You've got to find out what you really want. Promise me you'll keep trying, Julie. Promise me."

She tried to step around me. I stepped in her way again.

"Clarence, please. I don't want to be a dolphin."

I grabbed her by her arms.

"You think that's what this is about? That's not what this is about."

"Let me go, Clarence."

She tried to pull away, but I held her tight.

"Just a moment." I said. "Just... This is about you living for yourself, Julie. Finding out that you can't live your mother's life for her..."

And this was the crazy, unfortunate thing. The first time I ever saw Julie stand up for herself was when she stood up to me. She looked me right in the eye, and I swear I watched her, in that half-second, change from a little girl struck with hero-worship to a young woman, standing on her own two feet.

When she spoke, the words stung.

"I don't really see the difference whether I live her life or yours."

She'd completely misunderstood. And the clock was still ticking.

"I just want you to be free."

"So does Mother. Ask her."

A wave washed over her feet. I stepped back to avoid it.

There had to be a way to get through to her.

"You don't understand," I said. "She's a wonderful mother, right?"

Julie nodded evenly.

"She is."

"And you love her."

She nodded again.

"You love her so much that you can't do anything that would cause her pain."

That gave her pause.

"All right."

"You'd do anything for her…"

She pushed past me, and started up the beach.

I called after her.

"…anything. Can't you see what's happening to you? Yes. She's wonderful. Yes, you owe her everything."

I grabbed her from behind and spun her around.

"You love her so much you'd give up your dreams before you even see them. But that's wrong, Julie. Can't you see that? She's just like, like…"

My mind went blank. Julie narrowed her eyes.

"Like who?"

I couldn't think who, but I didn't have to. An ambulance pulled into the restaurant parking lot, its sirens screaming.

Julie pulled away from me, and stared in horror.

"Oh no," she breathed. "Mom!"

She ran toward the restaurant.

She was halfway up the beach before I realized why she was running. I called after her.

"Julie! It's all right! Stop!"

She stopped and turned, puzzled.

"Your mother's fine," I shouted. "They've come for me."

The ambulance had a logo on the side, over the words *North Hills Psychiatric Hospital*.

I took a step toward Julie, but my leg gave out under me, and I tumbled to the ground.

Julie rushed back, and helped me up.

"Are you okay?"

"Yeah, I said. It's just… my leg."

She helped me walk back to the parking lot where they were waiting. By the time we got there, the pain was better, but I had one hell of a limp.

Just like Charlie.

P icture this:
An ambulance sits in an empty parking lot. Two men, dressed in white, put a straitjacket on a third man. He wears shorts and a Hawaiian shirt. They slide the jacket over his arms, then make him turn around while they lace it up the back. One of the white-jacket men speaks to the man in straitjacket.

"How you been, Gabriel?"

The man in the straitjacket turns around again so they can cross his arms and pull the sleeves tight.

"Do I have to wear this, Jonesy?"

Jonesy smiles, pats him on the shoulder.

They put him in the back of the ambulance and start to close the door.

There's a house facing the parking lot, and a young woman comes running from the house, carrying a conch shell.

You know her. Her name is Julie.

"Wait a minute!" you say to Jonesy. "Please?"

Jonesy shrugs, stands aside.

Julie climbs in beside you.

"Thanks—for everything," she says. "You know. I wanted to say good-bye. I don't want to be a dolphin, but I do want to be like you."

She puts the conch down beside you.

"I hope you can understand this. You were willing to give up your freedom for me—you stayed, and tried to help, when you could have run. Well, I'm giving up my freedom for Mom—for her dream. You can understand that, can't you?"

She kisses you on the cheek. You'd like to hug her, but you can't move your arms, and for once in your life, you can't think of a thing to say.

Julie smiles at you, a little sadly.

"Maybe you did help me become a dolphin after all."

She flees to the house.

Jonesy swung the door closed, and hopped into the shotgun seat in front. The other guy started the engine, and circled the lot toward the exit.

Julie reached the house, just about the time we reached the road. I think she waved, but I couldn't see for sure.

The trees obscured my view.

THE DOLPHIN

21

A TERRIBLE MISTAKE

I had a hard time sitting up straight. It wasn't a normal ambulance. The "hospital" was run on a shoe-string, and everything about the operation suffered from that. The seat was a narrow shelf-like affair along one side, with a green plastic pad, which my shorts tended to slip on, and the ride was bumpy. I kept being thrown one way and another, and, because of the straitjacket, I couldn't use my hands to steady myself.

Julie's shell posed another problem. The bouncing slowly moved it toward the edge of the seat, and I couldn't reach out to grab it. I finally managed to push it back with one leg—my good one—although I nearly fell off the seat in the process, but I got it against the wall of the ambulance, about a foot and a half from me. It was resting on the curved side, but seemed to want to roll toward the wall, so it was stable enough.

I was sweating heavily by then from the exertion. It was a hot day to begin with, and straitjackets are not designed for comfort.

After a while, Jonesy called back to me.

"Been out to sea lately, Gabe?"

Jonesy was a nice enough guy, actually, but a bit of a smartass, and I really didn't feel like bantering with him at the moment.

"Not lately," I said.

Jonesy turned to the driver. The driver was a new guy, since my time in the hospital. I didn't know him.

"We're privileged characters, Al. You don't get to meet a dolphin in person every day. Ain't that right, Gabriel?"

I sighed.

"It was just a story, Jonesy—just a game I used to play."

"Just a game? Hey, Gabe! Maybe you're cured!"

"Yeah," I said, "Maybe I am."

Back at the house, Julie stood in front of her mirror, with a comb in her hair. She was supposed to be getting ready for the party, but the hand on the comb wasn't moving.

Ann appeared in the mirror, behind her.

"Only an hour left, honey."

Julie nodded, but the comb still didn't move.

"Do you think he'll be all right?" she asked.

Ann smiled reassuringly.

"Of course he will, honey. He's not bad, you know—just sick."

Jonesy put on a rock and roll station. Rock has a certain appeal —a basic, driving rhythm, like a beat of a heart, or the pounding surf. That afternoon, in the ambulance, it combined with the rhythm of the road and the heat to lull me into a sort of trance.

That's why I'm not sure whether I did the next thing on purpose.

I shifted my weight and slid down the wall so that I was lying on the seat, instead of sitting.

The part I'm not sure about is whether I intended to end up with my ear in Julie's conch.

I could hear the sea in that shell. My mind drifted through the past, putting memories together, making patterns, one way, then another.

I remembered a day at the beach with Charlie—I was nine or ten. He sat on an old, frayed, green beach towel. I sat next to him in the sand.

We worked on a sandcastle. Charlie used a little shovel to smooth one side of the castle. He was taking me through our private catechism.

"And what is Mrs. Jenson?"

I gave my standard sing-song response.

"A human."

"And Mr. Kettle, at the gas station?"

I cut little notches in the turret.

"A human."

"And the paperboy?"

He always kept it up until I started to giggle.

"A human."

Once I laughed he would move on.

"And me?"

I became serious again.

"A dolphin, Charlie."

"And you?"

I laughed.

"A dolphin, a dolphin, a dolphin, Charlie."

"And what's the difference between a dolphin and a human, Pup?"

I was vaguely aware of the ambulance, the music, the

straitjacket—but now I was tracking memories with crystal clarity.

I remembered Ann in her attic, talking about her mother, the hot scent of pine and the flickering light.

"She called this place—the restaurant and house—my 'legacy.'"

I remembered telling her about Charlie.

I remembered Charlie, dying in his bedroom.

"Promise me you'll follow your vocation. Be a Traveling Angel, Pup, like Dudley in the movie..."

I remembered him smoothing the sand with that rusted blue shovel.

"...the difference between a dolphin and a human, Pup?" he asked.

I cleared my young throat, even while I worked the turret with my Popsicle stick.

This was the important part.

"Humans live..."

I sat bolt upright in the ambulance. The memories came easily—I didn't need the shell anymore.

I remembered Ann, running her finger along the easel's edge.

"I'd promised Mother. It's too late for me."

I remembered Charlie, pouring milk into the jelly glasses.

"It's too late for me."

And Ann again.

"Julie's different. She can do it."

And Charlie.

"But you can. You're young—and strong."

The blue shovel had a little dent in its edge. It left a ridge in the side of the sandcastle.

"...the difference between a dolphin and a human, Pup?" he asked.

I cleared my throat.

"Humans live for…"

The ambulance slowed, pulling into a driveway.

Ann, in the attic, looked me squarely in the eyes.

"She's got more talent in her little finger…"

Charlie, weak in bed, gave a raw chuckle.

"You've got the touch, all right."

I came down the ladder to talk to Julie.

"You might be one of those who can do it."

Julie tried to get around me at the beach.

"I don't want to be a dolphin."

I cut another notch in the turret of our sand castle. The end of the Popsicle stick was stained red.

"And what's the difference between a dolphin and a human, Pup?"

I cleared my throat.

"Humans live for themselves, Charlie. Dolphins live for others."

Julie put the conch down beside me in the ambulance.

"Maybe you helped me become a dolphin after all."

The ambulance pulled to a stop. Rock and roll blared. The heat was unbearable; the strait jacket, uncomfortable.

I didn't care.

I had made a terrible mistake.

22

JULIE'S MOTHER

Danny Albright—the homeless kid I sent to Kels—was passing a tray of rumaki among the crowd on William Hogan's deck.

It's a small world.

Danny moved carefully, and with a certain grace, offering his tray to the guests who stood or sat in small groups, chatting over the combo that played quietly in the corner.

He couldn't believe his good fortune. A few weeks ago he had been homeless, jobless, broke.

Then he had met that crazy old man, not thirty feet from where he was standing at this very moment, and that had led him to Kels, who had not only given him a job, but helped him generally to get on his feet.

He had found a room to rent from a friend of Kels', and had actually impressed Kels with his work. And here he was, on a catering gig for Mr. Hogan, right back where it all started.

He wondered what had happened to the old guy who gave him the jacket.

He offered the tray to Mr. Hogan's sister. She was talking to a self-important fellow with a deep voice, who kept his chin pressed to his chest. She took one, and popped it into her mouth. The self-important character waved him off, and continued talking.

"Caterers?" he said, "At one of William's parties?"

Mr. Hogan's sister nodded, her mouth full.

In the kitchen, William was attempting to direct the caterers. He shot instructions in every direction, but was being completely ignored by the workers—who knew their business in the first place, and had their own boss to answer to in the second.

This, however, did not discourage William in the least.

"I want the glasses kept full," he shouted after a waiter who was carrying a bottle out to do just that.

And keep those hors d'oeuvres moving," he said to two more as they scurried past him with a tray in each hand.

"I want them eaten before they get cold," he shouted after them.

He stepped into the path of the next waiter, and sampled from his tray.

"Aren't these a bit salty?"

The waiter shrugged.

"You want to send them back?"

William considered.

"No," he said. "No. Go ahead. Nick! Nick?"

Nick materialized at his side.

"Why don't I take over in here," he said. "You've got enough to do."

William nodded.

"You're right. I need to see to my guests."

He stopped another waiter, and tasted a tiny quiche.

"I can't get caught up in these details, got to keep my balance."

He picked up a second quiche and thrust it at Nick.

"You think this is too dry?"

Nick put the quiche back on the waiter's tray and waved the man outside.

"Because you know," William said, "I'm really on a roll this time. I can feel it. Everything's just spinning along. I've just got to just keep the balance going."

William followed the waiter to the door, but stopped there and turned back.

"Nick!"

"Yes?"

"Has my lucky pen come back?"

Al, the ambulance driver, was not a man of deep thoughts.

He liked driving the ambulance. He liked driving in general. It was straightforward and uncomplicated work. You got the thing from point A to point B. Sometimes you got to use the siren and drive fast. Any problem you ran into was solvable, and the few times it wasn't, it really wasn't, and nobody blamed you.

He didn't mind working with Jonesy. Jonesy was basically a good sort—even if he was hard to understand. He seemed to be pretty bright most of the time, brighter than Al was. But then, sometimes, he would say really stupid things.

Like this morning, when they got the call on this Smith guy —the crazy in the back.

Jonesy said, "Did you know that some angels are dolphins, Al?"

What do you say to something like that? He didn't want to hurt Jonesy's feelings, so he just shrugged.

"No, I didn't."

Jonesy had laughed. That was another thing about Jonesy. He was always laughing for no reason.

Then he said, "Well, you're going to meet one today."

Al had just shrugged again. There was no point in talking about it, or trying to get Jonesy to see it was nonsense—he'd learned that long ago.

Later, when they had picked the guy up, Jonesy had tried to talk about it again, and even the Crazy had told him it was only a game. He guessed that was probably it. The Crazy had played this game with Jonesy, only Jonesy had thought it was for real.

He wondered, for a second, why Jonesy was in a white coat and the Crazy was the one in the straitjacket, if the Crazy knew it was a game, and Jonesy thought it was real. But that was a confusing line of thought, and he gave it up to concentrate on his driving.

Jonesy pointed to a hamburger stand in the middle of the village. Al nodded and pulled in.

Jonesy turned around in his seat, so he could see the Crazy. Al adjusted his mirror, to watch. The guy was staring into space, not moving a muscle. He'd seen them like that before, plenty of times. They'd probably have to carry him in when they got to the hospital.

But Jonesy just waved his hand in front of the Crazy's face, and yelled over the radio.

"I'm going to stop for lunch. You want a burger or something?"

The Crazy kind of shook his head; he looked right at Jonesy and smiled.

That was the thing, just when you thought Jonesy wasn't so bright after all, he surprised you.

"Hmm?" the Crazy said.

Jonesy repeated himself.

"You want a hamburger?"

"Oh. No, Jonesy. Thanks anyway, but I hate being hand-fed."

Jonesy thought about that for a moment, then swiveled his whole seat around and unfastened the jacket, so the guy could eat. That was the other thing about Jonesy. Sometimes he was nice.

The Crazy gave them a big grin.

"Cheeseburger and a Coke. Thanks."

Jonesy jumped out of the ambulance.

"The usual for you, Al?"

Al nodded.

"Just don't forget the fries, okay?"

He really liked his fries.

Ann hadn't been at William's party for five minutes when a very strange woman, wearing a skirt made out of a bunch of neckties, had introduced herself as "Celia-and-you-must-be-Julie's-mother-she's-such-a-nice-girl..." and had proceeded to alternate a non-stop monologue with a sort of relentless third degree for the better part of an hour.

Try as she might, Ann had not been able to pry herself away.

At the moment they were involved in the third degree, which seemed, somehow, to always reveal some important person that Celia knew, and would be all too happy to introduce to Ann.

"A restaurateur, are you?" she said, popping a small potato filled with caviar into her mouth. "Really? How wonderful! Have you met Kelsey? He runs the Seaside Bar and Grill."

Ann shook her head, searching her mind for an excuse to leave.

"He's catering this very party. Wait—I'll introduce you." She scanned the deck, and spotted Kels wedging himself out through the door from the house. She waved wildly, and shouted across the deck.

"Kelsey! Over here! It's Celia! I have someone you must meet!"

Even though everyone else heard this, Kels apparently didn't. His glance swept past them as though they weren't there. He suddenly seemed to remember something very urgent and squeezed his way back into the house in a great hurry.

Ann tried to become very small.

Celia patted her arm.

"Stay right here," she said. "I'll bring him over."

She threaded her way through the crowd. Ann breathed a sigh of relief, and searched the deck for a quiet corner, where she could sit alone for a moment.

But it was not to be.

A young woman about Julie's age accosted her before she had moved two feet, and it started all over again.

"Hello," she said. "You must be Julie's mother."

"Yes," Ann smiled, "But I'm afraid that at the moment I have to—"

The lovely young thing stuck out a hand.

"I'm Chris," she said.

Ann took the hand, her eyes on the door. She had to get away before Celia returned.

"Call me Ann," she said. "Why don't you walk with me?"

"I'm an old friend of Tim's, just back from Europe."

"Really?"

"Do you know where he is?"

23

MUST BE MAGIC

Al sat in the driver's seat of the ambulance, his cap pulled down low.

The radio blared Bruce Springsteen, and the heat of the day baked into his skin, making him drowsy. He liked the heat. He liked the driving beat of the song. He liked the way the inside of his hat smelled—a mixture of cloth and sweat. His finger tapped the gearshift lightly in time to the music.

The passenger door opened and closed. Jonesy was back.

Al yawned and reached up to tilt his cap back.

"You remember the fries this time?"

Jonesy didn't answer.

Al sat up, and looked around.

Jonesy wasn't in the ambulance. Puzzled, he looked over at the hamburger stand. Jonesy was there, still standing in line. A little ball of anxiety began to form somewhere at the base of Al's throat. He looked in his rear-view mirror.

The Crazy was gone.

He yanked his door open and jumped outside. Behind the ambulance, the Crazy was limping across the street.

For one of the few times in his life, Al wanted desperately to do something. He just couldn't figure out what. The lump of anxiety had sunk to the center of his chest now, and it was throbbing.

The Crazy was crossing the street, headed toward a bus that had stopped to take on passengers.

Al started after him, then stopped. He started to climb back in the ambulance, then changed his mind and got out again. He took a tentative step toward Jonesy, then backed up. He gawked, open-mouthed, at the Crazy again.

Finally, he decided to yell.

"Jonesy!"

Jonesy came running, juggling a bag of burgers and a tray of drinks. He almost dropped them, but managed to set them on the hood instead.

"What's wrong?"

Al pointed helplessly across the street, and Jonesy looked, just in time to see the Crazy disappear around the front of the bus. The driver closed the door, and the bus pulled away.

There was no one standing on the other side—only two women sitting on the bench, waiting for another bus.

Al swallowed.

"Where did he go?"

Jonesy gave him that strange look again. It always happened just before Jonesy said something really stupid.

"Gee, Al, I don't know. It must be magic."

Right. Magic.

Jonesy pushed past Al, into the driver's seat.

He waved Al around to the other side.

"Get in. You're riding shotgun."

Al got in. He didn't want to argue when Jonesy was acting strange like this.

They pulled out and fell in just behind the bus, which was going about five miles an hour. The bus wasn't getting away, but they weren't exactly catching it either.

Al had an idea.

"Should we use the siren?"

Jonesy gave him that strange look again.

"Oh, I think so, Al. This is going to be a real high-speed chase."

Julie had found a spot at the very edge of the party, where she could sit by herself, and not have to talk to people. She was tired of answering questions, and of thinking of questions to ask.

There was a slight breeze from the sea, and it cooled the back of her neck as she watched the crowd and wondered what was happening to Dudley/Clarence/Mr. Smith.

Across the deck, Tim was standing in a group of his friends, laughing, joking, like he belonged there. And he did. She just wasn't sure, somehow, that she did.

But it was too late to worry about that now.

She was just glad that he hadn't noticed she wasn't there. She didn't want to have to deal with all those new people right now.

A girl came up behind Tim, and put her hands on his eyes. He laughed and said something, then she said something back, and then he whirled around and gave her a hug.

Julie leaned forward, intent.

It was the girl from the picture in Tim's room.

There's an old joke Charlie taught me. You get someone to say "pots" four times, real fast. You get them to spell it. Then you get them to repeat it again. You do this for some time. "Pots, pots, pots, pots. P-O-T-S. Pots, pots, pots, pots." Then you say, "Quick! What do you do when you come to a green light?"

Nine times out of ten, they say, "Stop!"

They think you're trying to get them to say "pots," and they're so busy avoiding that mistake that they don't notice that a green light means *go*.

Jonesy and Al were so busy wondering where I could have gone to that it didn't occur to them that maybe I didn't go anywhere. I had rounded the front of the bus, walked right by the open door, and simply squatted down behind the bench at the bus stop.

The bus fumes almost did me in.

When I say "simply", I don't mean "easily". It was actually pretty difficult, considering my sudden leg problem.

It was even harder getting up. Once the ambulance had followed the bus, I grabbed the top of the bench with both hands, and, using only my good leg, managed to haul myself to my feet.

There was an old lady and a younger one sitting on the bench. They looked vaguely familiar. The older one peered up at me from under her purple hat and poked the younger one in the ribs.

"This is the man who helped me across the street the other night. Remember, dear? He knows how to treat a lady."

She winked at me.

The younger one, her daughter, was not pleased to see me. She gave me a social smile.

"We're eternally grateful."

She turned to look for the next bus. It was just a coincidence it put her back to me. The old lady poked at her again.

"You could learn a thing or two from him."

Al was back in the driver's seat. They had followed the bus to its next stop, and Jonesy had jumped out, telling Al to slide over. He waited patiently, happy to be behind the wheel again.

After a while, Jonesy came walking back, shaking his head.

"He wasn't there. Get on the radio. Ask the police for help."

Al reached for the microphone. Jonesy climbed in, still shaking his head.

"I don't get it," he said. "We were right behind it the whole way. I don't see how he could have got off."

Al mumbled to himself.

"Must be magic."

Jonesy looked at him sharply.

"What?"

Al shrugged.

"Nothing."

I was several blocks away by then, and had just turned off the main highway into a residential area. It was slow going. My leg throbbed mercilessly, even though I tried to carry all of my weight on the good one. The sweat poured off me, and not just from the heat.

Still, it was nice to be on a tree-lined street, out of the sun and traffic.

At least I was moving downhill, toward the beach.

About that time, Julie was sitting in her little corner of the deck, not thinking about me anymore at all. The sudden appearance of the girl from the picture had blown every thought out of her mind. All she could do was watch, mindlessly, as Tim and the girl talked, laughed, and teased each other.

Had she been able to think, she probably would have thought that the girl was very attractive, that Tim seemed to be happier than she had known him to be since they met. That Tim and the girl locked eyes in a way that she and Tim never had.

But none of these thoughts went through her mind. She just watched, mesmerized, thinking nothing.

This could have gone on forever, except for the tray of fruit.

It lowered in front of her, slowly, until the pineapple completely blocked her view.

She looked up, momentarily confused and still not thinking any real thoughts at all, to find herself looking into the eyes of the waiter who held the tray.

Danny smiled.

"Some fruit?" he asked.

Julie continued to stare. No words formed in her brain.

The waiter lowered the tray toward her hand.

"Try a grape."

Julie took one, mechanically, and pushed it between her lips. It was firm, and cool. She bit down and the juice—sweet, but not too sweet—cascaded over her tongue and down her throat. The skin was slightly bitter as she chewed it, setting off the flavor of the pulp.

The waiter was still smiling.

"How is it?" he asked.

Julie finished swallowing.

"It's... It's good."

The waiter nodded.

"Have a bunch."

Julie reached out, but her hand couldn't find the grapes without the help of her eyes, which refused to look away from his.

He laughed, and put a bunch in her hand.

24

SPINNING CONFIDENTLY

By then I had made it to the far end of William's street.

This gave me some satisfaction, but the final block felt like more than I could do. I hobbled across the parking strip and leaned against a van to give my leg a rest.

The scent of the sea was stronger here than it had been in town, and it mingled nicely with the perfume of fresh-cut grass. The next lawn over had the sprinklers on—not a smart move for the middle of a hot day, but I was grateful for the mist that drifted my way.

The pain in my leg was a searing electrical current, mixed with a strange numbness. I was breathing heavily.

At the end of the street, people were arriving for William's party. He had valets at the curb—dressed in tuxedos—to take the cars and park them. There was a van in the driveway like the one Kels used for catering.

While I leaned there, catching my breath, the front door opened on the house with the sprinklers.

I stood up, quickly, in case the van I was leaning against belonged to whoever was coming out. I limped back to the sidewalk.

It was a young mother with a little boy in tow. I recognized them immediately, and limped forward to say hello.

"Say, aren't you..." I said. "Didn't I...?"

The mother pulled the kid closer to her.

"Oh, yes," she said, "you saved my son from that skateboarder the other night. Nice to see you. I'm afraid we're running late."

She rushed the kid into their car.

As she fastened him into his car seat, the little squirt peered around her at me, then into his mother's face.

"You said he didn't save nobody from nothin'."

Julie had never noticed before just how silent Mr. Hogan's study was.

The four of them—Julie, her mother, Tim, and Mr. Hogan—had gathered there, just prior to announcing the engagement. Her mother was fussing with Julie's hair. Tim stood a few feet away, straightening his tie. Mr. Hogan paused from going over the contracts for the sale of the restaurant, to glance at the clock.

None of them said a word. Even the scent of the wood polish was heavy and silent.

She could see the waves breaking through the large picture window behind Mr. Hogan's head, but she couldn't hear them at all. She knew her heart was pounding in her chest, but she couldn't hear it either, or even feel it.

The only sound was the soft, almost imperceptible hum of the air conditioning.

When I finally limped into William's driveway, I was greeted by an attractively dressed woman with a little book in her hand.

She walked right up to me and smiled.

"Can I help you?"

I searched my mind for the right approach. A couple of waiters came around the side of the house, and passed us on their way to get something out of the van. I noticed absently that it had *Seaside Bar and Grill* painted on the side.

So it *was* Kels'.

The woman smiled some more.

"Are you on the guest list, perhaps?"

She flipped her little book open.

"If I could have your name?"

I smiled back, a little sheepishly.

"To tell the truth, ma'am, I'm probably not on that list. I'm an old friend of William's. I was in town and thought I'd just sort of drop in and surprise him."

I gestured vaguely at all the activity around us.

"I didn't know there was going to be a big party going on."

She smiled reassuringly.

"No problem. I'll send someone to check. Who shall I say…?"

I could feel that this approach was not going to work with her.

"Well," I said, "that would kind of ruin the surprise. Maybe if I just—"

But then something caught my eye.

William's house had a bay window in the front, and from where I was standing I could see the street I had just walked down, reflected in the side panes of the window.

There was an ambulance coming slowly down the street.

I recognized the ambulance. I even knew the names of the two guys in it, and who they were looking for.

I gave the lady my most convincing shrug.

"Maybe if I came back another time. Thanks anyway."

I turned to leave, and ran smack into a waiter. We sort of bounced off each other, and I started to apologize.

"Excuse me, I wasn't looking—Well, what do you know?"

It was the homeless kid. The one I sent to Kels.

He recognized me, too.

"Aren't you the guy who—"

But I didn't let him finish. That ambulance was getting closer.

I grabbed his arm, and pulled him toward the catering van.

"Could I have a moment of your time?"

In Mr. Hogan's study, the air conditioning hummed on.

Julie watched the breakers. Tim came over next to her, a little stiff in his suit, and took her hand.

She remembered having a bit part in the school play, during her junior year. She and some guy she hardly knew were cast as a couple, and were on stage for a total of about three minutes. All they did was stand in a corner and hold hands. They never said a single word to each other, through all the rehearsals, all of the performances—even at the cast party when it was all over.

Mr. Hogan cleared his throat.

"All right," he said. "That's umm... It's time to go out there, now. I'll make the announcement, if that's all right with everyone?"

He paused, and glanced at each of them.

"Fine. That's fine. And then... If any of you want to say anything in addition?"

He raised his eyebrows at Julie's mother. She shook her head.

"No?" he said, "Well, then, I'll make the speech, and then, let's allow..."

He glanced at his watch again.

"Oh... ten minutes for all the congratulations and everything, and then we can come back up here to sign the restaurant papers—keep everything spinning along nicely that way. After the signing we can just go back down and... and enjoy ourselves."

He nodded to himself and to them.

Julie wondered if she was supposed to say something.

Mr. Hogan nodded again.

"Fine, then... Everybody ready? Okay. Here we go."

In the ambulance, Al bobbed his head in time to the music, and let his eyes drift over the houses and the cars along the street. The trees, arching overhead, made a pleasant flicker of shadow and light as he eased the ambulance down the street.

Jonesy leaned forward next to him, peering tensely this way and that.

"Take it real slow, Al," he said. "We don't want to pass him by."

William led the little group out onto the deck, to the space he'd had Nick leave near the door for them to stand.

He was very pleased.

The price for the restaurant wasn't bad, considering it was a beachfront property—and with the impending marriage, the money wouldn't really be leaving the family anyway.

He lined the three of them up in a row. Ann gave her daughter's arm an excited little squeeze.

Yes. Things were going very well, finally.

He stepped in front of the others, and closed his eyes for a moment, imagining his little top, spinning confidently.

He cleared his throat.

"Could I have your attention please?"

The music stopped.

A few people looked his way. Nick picked up a glass and tapped it with a fork.

"Please?" William said. "Everybody? Thank you."

The crowd quieted down, and turned his way.

William cleared his throat again.

"Many of you may have been wondering exactly what the occasion of this celebration is. Well. I'm here to—to dispel the mystery, because the reason for this—this extravaganza, is the announcement that I am about to...

Sam, who was seated only a few feet away, his elbow propped on the back of his chair, shouted, "For God's sake, William. Just say it!"

The crowd laughed.

William nodded, smiled nervously, and started fresh.

"As most of you know, my nephew, Tim, has been visiting this month, and he's a very fine boy, though not always as punctual as I would like..."

He glanced back at Tim. But it was Julie who caught his eye. For some reason he found himself thinking that she didn't look happy.

He shook off the thought and continued his speech.

"Well, while he's been here, he's managed to meet a wonderful young—"

"Excuse me."

It was one of the waiters.

William smiled, thinking that there would be hell to pay for this guy after the party.

The waiter continued.

"I'd like to say a few words before you begin."

There he stood, in his white uniform, holding a tray of hors d'oeuvres, square in the center of the deck, tables of guests on all sides of him.

And he was asking to make a speech.

William revised his opinion.

This would have to be dealt with right now. The only question was how to do it without ruining the moment.

He looked the man over carefully, trying to decide how to handle him.

"Would that be all right?" the waiter asked, and then he continued, "William?"

A red top wobbled irretrievably through William's brain.

His mouth dropped open, then closed again, and finally he managed to speak.

"Dudley?"

ANNOUNCEMENTS

Announcements have a lot of power.

A politician is just a politician until he announces that he's running for president—then suddenly he's a candidate. People rally around him, donate money, volunteer their services to help him win.

If you announce your graduation from high school, people send you gifts.

What's a business advertisement but a kind of announcement? Someone announces they'll sell widgets at ten percent off, and customers flock to their door, as if by magic.

But there are two sides to everything.

You'd better have those widgets in stock if you want to keep those customers, and you'd better be willing to honor the price you promised.

If you don't actually graduate from high school, you're in for some pretty embarrassing moments, talking to the people who sent you gifts. And a politician who announces, but backs out too soon, may have committed political suicide.

Once you announce a wedding, it's a lot harder to back out of it.

Danny lent me the waiter's uniform and got me into the party with a tray of hors d'oeuvres. We discussed some contingency plans on the way. I worked my way to the center of the deck just in time to interrupt the announcement.

I knew William wasn't pleased, but there was no choice.

I began by addressing all the guests, who stared like I was a circus act.

"I find myself in a rather awkward position," I told them. "I did something today that this young lady—"

I gestured toward Julie.

"—that this young lady thought was very noble. But it wasn't noble at all, and I'd just like to straighten that out with her."

I looked Julie in the eyes. This part was going to be difficult, but it had to be said.

"I didn't stay because I was putting you first, Julie. I thought that was why I stayed, I told myself it was, but it wasn't. I realized that a little while ago, and I want you to understand, before..."

My leg began to tingle as well as ache. I wet my lips and continued.

"I stayed, Julie, to try to get you to do something for *me*."

Jonesy grabbed Al's arm, and pointed down the tree-lined street.

"Pull over here."

He meant by the house with the valets out front.

"I want to talk to these guys."

Al pulled over.

He thought those guys were probably pretty uncomfortable, dressed like that.

Also, he was getting hungry.

Julie looked me right in the eyes. She wasn't accusing me. She didn't seem sad or happy or—or anything.

I struggled on.

"You remember that virus I told you about once, when we were sitting around telling stories? Well, I think I know what that virus really is."

I became aware of the crowd around us, listening to all this, and I turned to them again.

"This has got to seem very strange to you people. I want you to know I understand that."

They continued to stare, their mouths hanging open.

I met Julie's eyes again.

"Somewhere," I said, "a long way back, one of us wasn't able to live out a dream."

Al tapped his fingers on the steering wheel while Jonesy talked to the valet. He wondered how long this was going to take. He didn't mind sitting around, but Jonesy had turned the radio off.

Al liked to listen to music while he waited.

After a while Jonesy stuck his head in the window.

"Pull it up ahead and park it, Al. This may take a while."

Al nodded.

At least it was something to do.

I held Julie's eyes with mine, willing her to understand.

"One of us," I said, "wasn't able to live out his dream—or maybe her dream. And I think this person wanted this dream so badly that he—or she—asked his children to live it for him."

I was pretty sure she understood me. I shifted the tray of

hors d'oeuvres from one hand to the other, to take some of the strain off my leg.

"Oh, I don't think he asked them in so many words. He probably never said a thing about it—maybe not even to himself. But they knew what he wanted, even if they couldn't say it either, and I think they loved him so much that they tried to do it—they tried to live his dream for him, just like I did with Charlie."

I glanced around at the guests again. They needed a little more explanation.

"I was raised," I told them, "by a wonderful old codger, and I would have done just about anything he asked me to."

Catatonic.

I turned back to Julie.

"But it was Charlie's dream, Julie, and no matter how much I wanted to, or how much I tried to, I couldn't make it mine. That's what Charlie never understood."

Al pulled ahead to the spot Jonesy had pointed at, and eased the ambulance into place. Then he leaned across the passenger seat and adjusted the outside mirror so he could watch Jonesy talk to the valet.

He wondered if it would be all right to turn the radio back on.

Jonesy was through with the valet. He walked toward the house and talked to a woman who stood just outside the front door.

It was way past lunch time.

Al was curious whether Jonesy realized that the burgers and fries had fallen off the hood when they pulled out to chase that bus. He couldn't be sure.

Jonesy was not always so good at noticing things.

He decided he could turn the radio on, if he kept it real low. He turned the knob slowly until it clicked. Then he looked in the mirror, and turned it off again.

Jonesy was running toward the ambulance.

"Al!" he shouted, "call for backup! We're going in!"

That was okay with Al.

Maybe they'd get some food.

"But if Charlie had understood," I told Julie, "if Charlie had known what a mistake it was for me to follow his dream, he wouldn't have wanted me to, because all the time I was trying to live his dream, my own dream was locked up inside of me, suffocating, until I was willing to do anything to make it real. Anything.

"People have lots of dreams in a lifetime, Julie. Some you live, and some you don't. But they have to be yours.

"My dream, finally, was just to be free of Charlie's dream—to go home. The more I pushed it down, the stronger it got, until it couldn't stay down anymore."

I noticed Ann. She watched Julie closely, with a strange look on her face.

I kept on.

"And the pressure just kept building, Julie. It got so I felt if I couldn't break free—if I couldn't go back—then someone had to. I decided that someone was you."

Julie's eyes were clear, but her lower lip trembled a little.

"If I couldn't escape Charlie's plans for me, I'd break you free of your mother's plans for you. If I couldn't go home, go back to being a... then maybe you could..."

I sensed something moving behind me. I turned a little, and

caught a glimpse of Jonesy and Al, reflected in the windows of the house. They were closing in on me.

But that didn't matter anymore. All that mattered was Julie. I had so little time to undo all the damage I had done.

"...maybe you could go home for me," I said.

"I was wrong, Julie. I was just as wrong as Charlie had been about me. You'd have ended up like I did, missing out on your own life, and then forcing it on someone else..."

Al and Jonesy were sneaking up behind me, working their way through the crowd. There wasn't any time left.

"I can't tell you what to do now, Julie. I wouldn't dare. I just came to tell you that I'm not living Charlie's dream anymore. I'm going to live my own, or try to, anyway."

I turned my attention to the catatonic guests.

"That's all I came to say." I told them, "You've been very patient, and I want to thank you for that."

Did you ever see a bunch of fish lined up, staring out through the glass wall of an aquarium?

26

THE GOOD-LOOKING ONE

I waited for Julie to say something—anything. But she was silent. She didn't even nod.

I had tried. The rest was up to her. Like I said, I couldn't presume to know.

"Go ahead, William," I said. "Make your speech."

I was surprised he had let me make mine.

Al and Jonesy were closing in on either side of me, but I didn't care anymore. My leg was killing me.

William took a moment to come to life again.

"Well," he said, and looked around uncertainly. "Well, as I—as I was saying... before this..."

Al reached me first and put his hand on my arm.

"Don't," Julie said. "Please."

But she wasn't talking to Al. She was talking to William.

William looked a little dizzy. He paused, puzzled.

Julie took a deep breath, and patted Tim's hand before letting it go. She looked him in the eyes.

"I'm sorry Tim, I can't do this."

William was looking at me.

"Why," he said, "am I not surprised by this?"

Suddenly, I felt differently about my friends Al and Jonesy.

Suddenly I cared whether they dragged me back to a locked ward and sedation.

Suddenly I cared very much.

I turned to Al, offering the tray I had been balancing the whole time.

"Would you like an hors d'oeuvre?" I asked.

Al hesitated, then reached out to take one.

"Have all you want," I said.

And I handed him the tray.

He grabbed it with one hand, had trouble balancing it, and let go of my arm to grab it with the other.

I limped toward the house.

Jonesy snapped at Al as he pushed past him.

"Put that thing down!"

Al looked around in panic, then handed the tray to one of the catatonic guests.

By the time I reached William, Jonesy had half caught up to me. I wasn't moving very fast.

I clapped a hand on William's arm as I passed him.

"Thanks, William," I said.

I meant it.

Jonesy was right behind me. I decided it was probably all over.

And then a curious thing happened.

I pushed past Julie and Ann and Tim on my way through the door into the house, and looked back at Jonesy, hot on my trail.

He was just passing William.

If I hadn't seen it with my own eyes...

William stuck his foot out.

Jonesy pitched to the floor.

And Al fell on top of him.

Al decided that Jonesy was confused again.

As soon as they fell, Jonesy had pushed him off, struggled to his feet, and shouted "Get up, you idiot!" like it was Al's fault. But Jonesy had fallen first, so Al couldn't see how *he* had caused it.

No. Jonesy was mixed up. He was pretty sure of that.

Then Jonesy had pointed at the house, and shouted, "Come on. He went through there!"

They ran through the living room, around the corner, through the dining room, and into the kitchen.

Al thought it was a real nice house.

The side door, leading outside from the kitchen, was just slamming shut.

They dashed across the kitchen and out through the door, in time to see a white pant leg disappear around the front of the house.

They reached the front of the house just as their prey leapt into the catering van.

Jonesy took two running steps toward the van, but it was too late—the engine leaped into life, and the van began to move. He turned and sprinted toward the ambulance.

Al watched him for a second, puzzled, then followed.

"Jonesy?" he called out, "don't you want to—"

But Jonesy interrupted him.

"Damn it, Al. Just shut up and get in the ambulance."

He was already starting the engine.

Al shrugged and climbed in.

Julie followed the ambulance guys as far as the kitchen. Her mother and Mr. Hogan were right behind her. She closed the side door and turned around to look at them.

The room was full of warm, rich food smells, but empty, for the moment anyway, of caterers.

Her mother gazed past her, through the window in the side door.

She sighed.

"I hope they catch him."

Julie felt a sudden surge of anger.

"I don't."

Her mother's eyes snapped to hers, surprised.

Julie thought for a moment she was going to get a lecture, but Ann just nodded.

Al hunched in the passenger seat of the ambulance, confused. He didn't understand Jonesy at all.

"Jonesy," he said.

Jonesy didn't even glance his way.

"Shut up."

That was the problem. He had tried to ask a couple of times, but Jonesy had just kept telling him to shut up. So it wasn't his fault. But he couldn't help worrying, anyway.

It was just possible Jonesy hadn't noticed.

The guy in the catering van hadn't been limping.

Outside, through the kitchen window, Julie could see Tim on the deck. He sat with the girl from the photo. They talked intensely, in a world of their own.

"Did you see where that guy went who was here earlier," Julie asked, "the one who was serving the grapes?"

The girl from the photo put a hand on Tim's arm.

"Grapes?" Ann asked, "Are you hungry, dear?"

Julie laughed.

"The good-looking one—the guy, I mean."

Ann stiffened. "Julie!"

"Oh, he'll be back."

The door into the dining room was open. The voice came from behind it—between the door and the wall.

It swung closed, revealing an old friendly face.

I grinned and stepped forward.

"He'll be back," I said again.

"He's running a little errand for me."

The catering van skidded around the turn from the main highway onto a mountain road.

Danny glanced in the rearview mirror and laughed.

The ambulance was right behind him.

The music played again.

Guests had recovered from their catatonic state. The air was filled with their chatter. The perfume of food and wine mixed with the scent of sea breeze over hot sand.

I leaned against the railing at the end of the deck, where Julie, Ann, William, and I had taken ourselves for a bit of privacy.

I was saying goodbye.

Julie hugged me.

"I was right in the ambulance, you know. You did risk everything to help me, after all. And coming back here, when you could have just run away, proves it."

I grinned.

"You think you're very clever. But I came back to straighten something out between us—not for Charlie. You remember that."

I grasped William's hand.

"Good-bye, my friend."

He was close to tears.

"Let me know where to call you," he said.

"If I can."

Ann stood behind William. I stuck a hand toward her.

"Thanks for everything."

She shook it briefly, and let go.

"I can't say I won't be glad to get back to normal, Clarence, but I do wish you luck."

William raised his eyebrows.

"Clarence?" he said.

"Where will you go?" Julie asked.

I shrugged.

"I can't get home just yet, but I'll find a place where I can keep trying."

She knew what I meant.

I pecked her on the cheek, and turned toward the stairs at the end of the deck.

There stood my old friend, Officer Barnes.

He held a gun.

27

THE COLOR OF THE SEA

Officer Barnes smiled.

"Hi, Clarence. Just put your hands on the railing."

Julie gasped.

"No! You can't!"

This was where I was supposed to say, "No, Julie, it's all right," and go quietly.

Only I didn't feel like going quietly.

But I didn't feel like doing anything daring, either.

What I did was take a step backward.

The officer took a step forward.

"Come on," he said. "Don't make this difficult."

I took another step back, and found my butt against the railing. For a brief second, I imagined myself leaping over the railing and running.

Then I remembered my leg.

Barnes stepped forward again.

He pulled out his handcuffs.

He reached for my arm.

I can't explain what happened next.

I had been taken in many times before. I knew the drill. It

wasn't pleasant, but it wasn't life-threatening. It certainly wasn't anything that should have caused the kind of unearthly panic I felt at that moment.

That panic welled up inside of me, rooting itself in my deepest fears, worse than anything I had felt before, worse than anything I had imagined. It felt like those handcuffs were the end of me, the end of my world, the end of everything I ever loved.

It began deep in my bowels, and worked its way upward, through my solar plexus, through my lungs and shoulders, through my back and my throat. It came out of my mouth in a single shattering tone somewhere between a moan and a scream —a deafening mountain of sound aimed right at Officer Barnes' face.

It was the first time I had used a dolphin blast in at least thirty years—the first time ever out of the water.

The good officer staggered to the floor.

I put a tentative hand to my mouth, then laughed—first timidly, then with a great, head-tilted-back roll of relief that came from almost as deep a place as the blast itself.

Ann and William rushed to Barnes' side.

Julie stared wide-eyed, first at him, and then at me.

"It's all right," I said. "He'll be fine in a minute."

All the guests were looking our way again. Celia ambled toward us in her necktie skirt.

"I've got to go," I said. "Now."

I limped past them, and down the stairs to the beach.

Julie called after me.

"Do you need a ride or something?"

I laughed again.

"No," I said. "I think I may have my own transportation after all."

My leg was feeling better already.

Some people say that everyone and everything in the universe is all connected, all working together somehow.

I wouldn't know.

I do know that before I had gone ten feet, I heard a dolphin calling, out beyond the breakers.

It was no one I knew, but she had a beautiful voice.

The music and chatter from William's party drifted after me. I pulled off the bow tie from the caterer's uniform and tossed it on the sand.

I stopped for just a second to rub my leg. It felt a lot better.

I let my eye follow the water out to where it met the sky, cloudless and the palest yellow. I was surprised.

It was almost sunset.

A pelican circled, then plummeted after a fish.

I pulled off my shoes and socks and strolled toward the sea.

I could see her now—my dolphin friend—leaping into the air, quick, clean, and alive, and then plunging back into the waves.

William watched Officer Barnes sip water from a glass Celia held to his lips.

William was concerned, but the officer did seem to be recovering nicely.

And there was business to deal with.

He turned to Ann.

"We still need to sign that contract, you know."

Ann nodded absently, but Julie grabbed her mother's arm.

"We need to talk," she said.

She pulled Ann to one side, just out of hearing. They began an intense conversation.

William rolled his eyes.

His top was wobbling once again.

I strode along confidently, my limp completely gone.

My friend beyond the breakers had been joined by two more.

There was no mistaking it. They were calling to me.

I began to jog, past sunbathers, past surfboards and beach umbrellas, peeling my shirt off as I ran, the sand hot on my bare feet. I pushed myself faster and faster, fastening on the sea with my mind, trying to reel it in by sheer will-power, straining till I thought I would burst.

Nothing else mattered. Nothing.

Ann and Julie approached William looking timid and apologetic. He laughed wryly—at least that was the effect he had in mind.

"Don't bother to explain," he said. "You've changed your mind again."

Ann gave him a sad smile.

"Julie wants to run the restaurant herself."

I stopped at the waterline to pull off my slacks. The water was freezing, in spite of the heat, and the salt wind cooled my face and chest.

I glanced back at the party. I couldn't hear the music anymore, just the breakers. A group of sand-pipers retreated as a wave washed over the sand, then followed as it flowed out again.

I stood still, letting it wash over my feet.

I thought of Charlie. I couldn't blame him. I'd known him—and his intentions—too well. But I couldn't understand him anymore, either. I could no longer fathom how he could prefer a fantasy of wings and a halo to the cold, deep reality of the sea, to smooth gleaming skin, to the solid ripples of muscle underneath, to the rush of water past my ears.

I couldn't imagine trading reality for fantasy, love for mere benevolence, self-knowledge for self-importance. Maybe it wouldn't have been that way for him, but that was how it had been for me. And I couldn't wait to leave it behind.

The sea beyond was alive with dolphins, now, thousands of them, calling over the roar of the surf.

And before I hit the water, I knew.

I knew it was going to happen.

Before William could say anything, Julie stepped forward.

"I'm going to run the restaurant," she said, "But I'd like to offer you a job."

He almost laughed.

"A job?"

She was serious.

"Now Clarence is gone I'm going to need a chef."

William was astonished.

"A chef? Hmm. A chef. Well, that's very... I'd have to..."

He paused for a moment to consider, then raised an eyebrow.

"How much does it pay?"

I waded out to my waist and slipped out of my shorts. This time I could feel it. This time I had it right.

I let the air out of my lungs.

I smiled.

I dropped under the waves.

The sounds turned to light the instant I hit the water.

I didn't have to do a thing.

It took me over. It turned me inside out. It filled me with hope and with life and with pain.

It ran through my body like magic.

Like time.

Like the color of the sea.

Picture this:

Sea and sky, as far as the eye can see. Clouds tinged with sunset, air tinged with salt, the lap of a wave, the cry of a gull.

Silence.

A woman steps out of a house by the sea.

She glances across the parking lot, at her daughter's restaurant, but goes directly to a large canvas-covered object on her deck.

She removes the canvas, revealing a fine old studio easel.

She sits.

And she begins to paint.

...The Beginning

(If you enjoyed this book, go to krwatts.com/TGD-P for your free copy of another book by K. R. Watts.)

ACKNOWLEDGMENTS

This story has a long history. It started as a screenplay, was rewritten as a stage play, reworked again as a different screenplay, serialized as a novel, and rewritten once more in its present form over a period of decades.

My thanks to all of the people who have read it in its various incarnations, given me feedback, encouraged me, or contributed in many ways. I'm not going to name you all, mostly because its been so long, and there are so many of you, that I would inevitably leave someone out and be miserable about that.

I would, however, like to mention two people whose help was absolutely critical: Mike Rhodes, whose interest in a very different story was the spark that ignited this one, and David Malley, whose insightful input on one of the story's incarnations as a screenplay ended up greatly improving the early part of the current book.

Beyond that, I'll only mention Virginia, for infinite reasons, to whom this book is dedicated.